THE ICE CREAM KID

Brain Freeze!

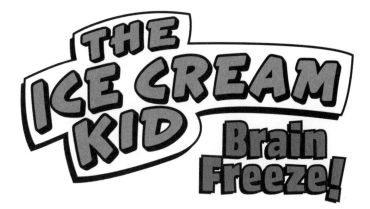

THE ICE CREAM KID Brain Freeze!

Todd Clark

Andrews McMeel Publishing®

Kansas City • Sydney • London

Dedicated to my amazing family
With thanks to God, Jason, Sheila, and t

CONTENTS

CHAPTER 1

GOOD MORNING

You ever wake up with one half your brain totally psyched and the other half completely frozen by fear? Weird, huh? Well, good morning, Friday! I decided right away to focus on the cool stuff happening today—not the stupid after-school thing my big mouth got me into.

Okay, so you're probably wondering who is this split-brained weirdo? I'm Irwin Snackcracker, and I'm heading into the kind of day fourth graders dream about. Well, fourth-grade boys at least. Can't speak for the girls; besides, they talk enough on their own—"Blah, blah, blah. Giggle, giggle,

giggle." I'm sure there are other things in there also, but that's what boys mostly hear.

Anyhow, one half of today was going to be epic: pizza and tater tots for lunch in the cafeteria, plus a grossest booger contest with the guys at recess. I jumped out of bed, leaped over a mountain of stinky clothes, shot a basketball into an open dresser drawer, kicked a soccer ball out of the way, and ran to the bathroom. I checked both nostrils,

HE LEAPS THE STINK AND SCORES!

UNREALISTICALLY
CLEAN KID'S
BATHROOM FLOOR

shining a flashlight up there for proper exploration. Nothing too promising yet, but it was still early. No need to panic.

I was halfway down my banister slide when Mom yelled at me to come down for breakfast. She was gonna freak! It usually took her at *least* five "I MEAN IT, MISTERS!" before my butt was at the table and ready to eat. Mom

turned and saw me sitting there, dressed, ready, and smiling. My hair even looked sort of presentable, meaning it wasn't sticking out in five different directions. Mom just looked at me kind of shocked. She kept yelling for me anyway, out of habit. Then she cautiously slid a bowl of oatmeal in front of me, covered her ears, and waited for my usual high-pitched whining about the evils of oatmeal and how the Quaker Oats guy looks like someone from the *Stranger Danger* video we watched in first grade.

I just looked at the bowl, smiled, and asked, "Could I perhaps have just a smidge of brown sugar to liven it up a bit?" I used my awesome British accent, which makes *everything* hilarious and NEVER gets old or annoying.

Then I ate up all the oatmeal.

"Who are you? And what have you done with Irwin?" asked Mom.

I just looked up and sweetly replied, "Boy, I'd better hustle so I've got time to properly brush *and* floss."

My mother fainted. Wham!

After brushing my teeth and one last nostril check, I headed back downstairs. Mom was still on the floor from her fainting. I asked her if she was okay, and she smiled and gave me a thumbs-up, so I leaped over her, grabbed my backpack, and shot out the door. Other than the slight hiccup with the oatmeal for breakfast (Pop-Tarts would have

been my first choice), it was a perfect day. Man, the sun

was even shining. I quickly met up with my best buddy, Trey,

and we strode off toward the Mock City School, home of

the Screaming Bigfoots . . . or Bigfeet. Either way it's a weird mascot.

Trey was cool and smart. He didn't talk a lot, which was fine. Boys mostly communicate through throwing things, punching shoulders, and burping anyhow.

"What's up?" Trey asked.

"Nothin.'"

"Did you see that thing on that channel?" he continued.

"Totally," I replied, even though I had NO idea what Trey was talking about.

This was a normal conversation for us. We avoided talking about stuff like school, family, and anything we ever actually cared for other than sports. It kept things simple.

Up ahead we could see our friend Elisha coming out her front door . . . *skipping*. WHO SKIPS AT 8:15 IN THE MORNING?!

Elisha does.

Mom once told me her enthusiasm was contagious. That always freaked me out. I thought the flu was contagious.

Anyhow, me and Trey and Elisha have been friends FOREVER. Like since kindergarten, back when we were kids. Trey and I still owed Elisha because when we were first graders she saved us from a nasty bully . . . *Wendy C.*

Unlike Trey and me, Elisha talked a lot . . . A WHOLE LOT. I had found through studies in the field that most girls do talk a lot . . . and giggle . . . and then talk about how fun it was to giggle . . . and then put things in their hair. And then talk about how cute the things in their hair look. I've given up trying to figure girls out. It made my head hurt, and everyone knows that heads were made to put baseball caps on, nothing more.

"Hi, friendboys!" Elisha started talking as soon as she saw us.

Trey and I just looked at each other. Neither one of us really wanted to reply . . . but I couldn't take it.

"What's a 'friendboy'?" I asked.

"Well, Mr. Crankypants, you guys are boys," Elisha replied.

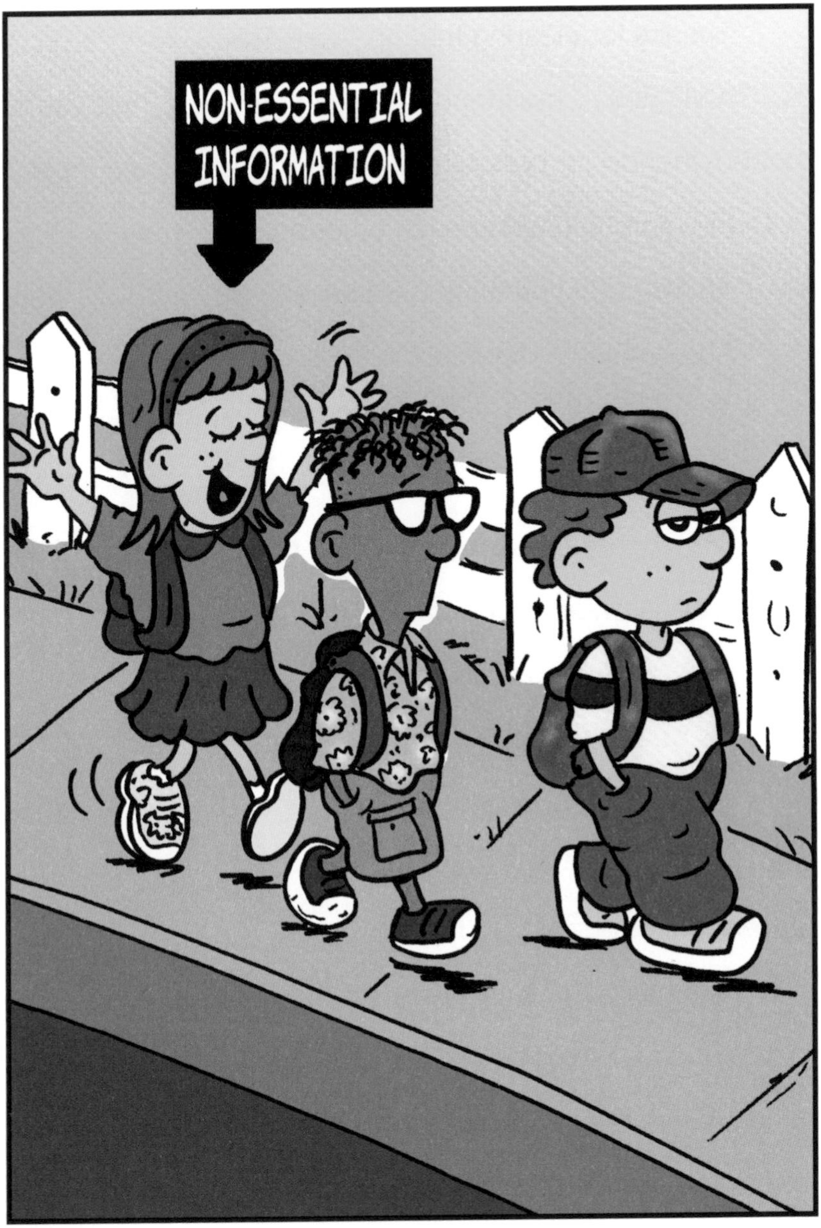
NON-ESSENTIAL
INFORMATION

"Thanks for clearing that up," said Trey.

"AND you're my friends," Elisha continued, "but you're not boyfriends, so I've come up with the word *'friendboys'*!"

Trey and I looked at each other again.

"So, what do you think?" Elisha asked.

"About what?" I replied.

"About the word 'FRIENDBOYS'?!" she yelled. "Pay attention."

Sometimes Trey knew just what to say to Elisha: "If we say that it's genius, can we move on?"

"Yes," answered Elisha.

"It's genius," Trey said.

"I know. There, now you two can get back to whatever you were discussing. Boogers, or baseball, or baseballs covered in boogers," said Elisha.

As far as girls go, however, Elisha was *okay*. If I DID like girls, **which I don't**, I guess she'd be all right. But I don't like them. We're clear on that, right? Besides, seeing Elisha reminded me of the dreaded part of today. You see,

Elisha was fast—I mean, really fast. Like, she could beat all the boys in a race, even in her sneakers that had flowers and kitties on them, which made losing to her twice as embarrassing.

Anyhow, I had shot my big mouth off about how I could beat her in a race if I *really* tried. Which was stupid since I'm one of the slowest kids in my class. Ronnie Herzog challenged me on it and dared me to race her. My reputation as a dude was at risk. We even made a bet. If I won, Ronnie had to tell our teacher in front of the whole class he had made poopie in his pants and needed to be excused. If I lost, I had to kiss Elisha—right on the face! AND tell her I loved her! AAUUGGHH! Not ready for that!

Elisha had no idea about the bet, and I put it out of my mind for now. I was just glad she didn't bring up the race as we walked to school.

The three of us walked through the front doors of school like we owned it, but not in a snotty way. We were just in a good place in life: way past the awkward kindergarten and first-grade years, where the threat of a thumb-sucking slip was still a scary possibility, but not yet an old kid—the ones recently attacked by the Zit Fairy. EWWW. And the last feather in our caps . . . the school nurse, Ms. Scabs, had recently declared us all "cootie free."

CHAPTER 2

THE CONTEST

After a pretty regular morning in Ms. Frost's class of algebra, geometry, spelling, re-creating the entire Civil War out of toothpicks, reading seventy-four chapters in our English book, and making a volcano that actually worked, it was time for lunch. (In case you hadn't noticed, Ms. Frost liked to keep the class busy.)

The lunch line seemed to take forever . . . the smell of square pizza slices and unwashed hairnets was killing me! I made a note to myself to create a room deodorizer that smelled like this someday.

Another million in the bank.

Me and Trey found our regular spot in the cafeteria: far enough from the youngsters so as not to be confused for one, but not too close to the fifth graders who could reach you with a flung pea. Those dudes were deadly accurate.

Lunch was perfect. The pizza had plenty of pepperonis, and each was filled with a glistening pool of grease. The tater tots were made to order: slightly burnt on the outside with a nearly frozen core. Man! Those lunch ladies could cook!

Well, most of them.

There was a rumor about some lunch lady years ago whose cooking actually killed some kids! They say she lurks in the halls during fire drills and assemblies, but I don't believe it. Other people say she's out prowling the streets of Mock City, waiting for revenge for getting fired. But come on, you kill a couple kids with your meat loaf, you probably deserved at *least* a trip to the principal's office.

The bell rang for the after-lunch recess. Me and the other boys raced outside. We met at the monkey bars for the grossest booger contest . . . well, first we *pretended* our fingers were loaded with snot and raced at the herd of girls talking by the swings. The girls ran and screamed, "GROSS!" and "STOP IT!"

Good times!

The booger contest itself went okay. I came in third with a pretty respectable pick. I was probably lucky to get the bronze considering I got a pretty bad index (digger) finger cramp during my initial entry and was forced to call a time-out for injury. Jimmy Trowbridge won the contest with an absolute gem of a booger. The thing was as long as your thumb and chock-full of dirt, pencil shavings, and what we were all pretty sure was a live snail. The kid was an artist . . . or athlete . . . whatever.

Since today was Friday, there was one last order of business: *ice cream*. Our school sold ice cream on Fridays as a fundraiser. No one was sure *what* the money they raised went for. My guess was that it went toward those fancy cars the teachers drove. Ms. Frost's car was called a "Pinto" and even had one door that was a different color from the rest of the car. Must have cost a fortune to customize it like that. Pimp my Pinto.

I never knew if my mother had remembered to give me ice cream money or not. I had stopped asking because Mom wasn't too thrilled with the whole sticky-sweet program to begin with, but she often would just put quarters in my pants pockets on Fridays to be nice. I hadn't checked yet this morning. I closed my eyes and made a wish.

"Boogers and burps, London and France,

Let me find money down in my pants."

I dug deep into my front pocket. And just past what felt like half of an old Oreo . . .

SCORE! TWO QUARTERS! HOORAY FOR MOM!

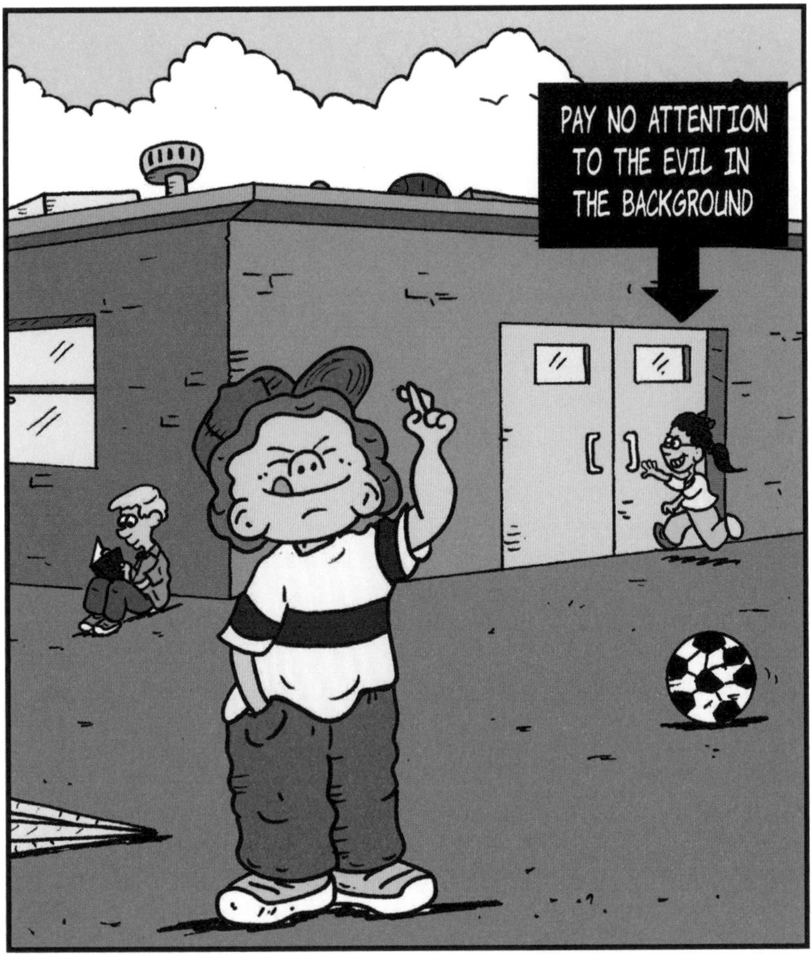
PAY NO ATTENTION
TO THE EVIL IN
THE BACKGROUND

CHAPTER 3

SQUIRREL CHAT

I hustled over to the little ice cream cart inside the corner of the cafeteria. I hoped there was still a good selection. The booger contest, although enjoyable and character building, had taken up a lot of recess.

There was one person in line, Wendy C., the bully from first grade. (She thought it sounded cool just to go by an initial.) Anyway, one person on an ice cream line was good and bad. A short line meant "no waiting," but it also could mean "no good ones left."

I walked up and got in line behind Wendy C. I asked the ice-cream guy about the selection. Mr. NO RUNNING! (not his real name, just all he ever said) grunted. Wendy C. was halfway down inside the cart. She screamed, "The last fudgesicle!" and came up beaming. Then she did that stupid hair flip she always does and smacked me in the face with her ponytail and all the stupid things clipped to it. She made a motion like she was going to punch me. I flinched. She won.

"Good luck . . . *Irwin*," Wendy C. said as she strolled away. I didn't have time for a snappy comeback. I usually never had one anyway. Mr. NO RUNNING! popped open the cart's lid, and I peered down inside. Just ice cream sandwiches, kind of what I expected. Oh well, it would have to do. An ice cream sandwich is better than NO ice cream at all.

But right when I was digging for my quarters, I saw what appeared to be a slightly different color of paper buried in the far corner of the cart. Could it be . . .

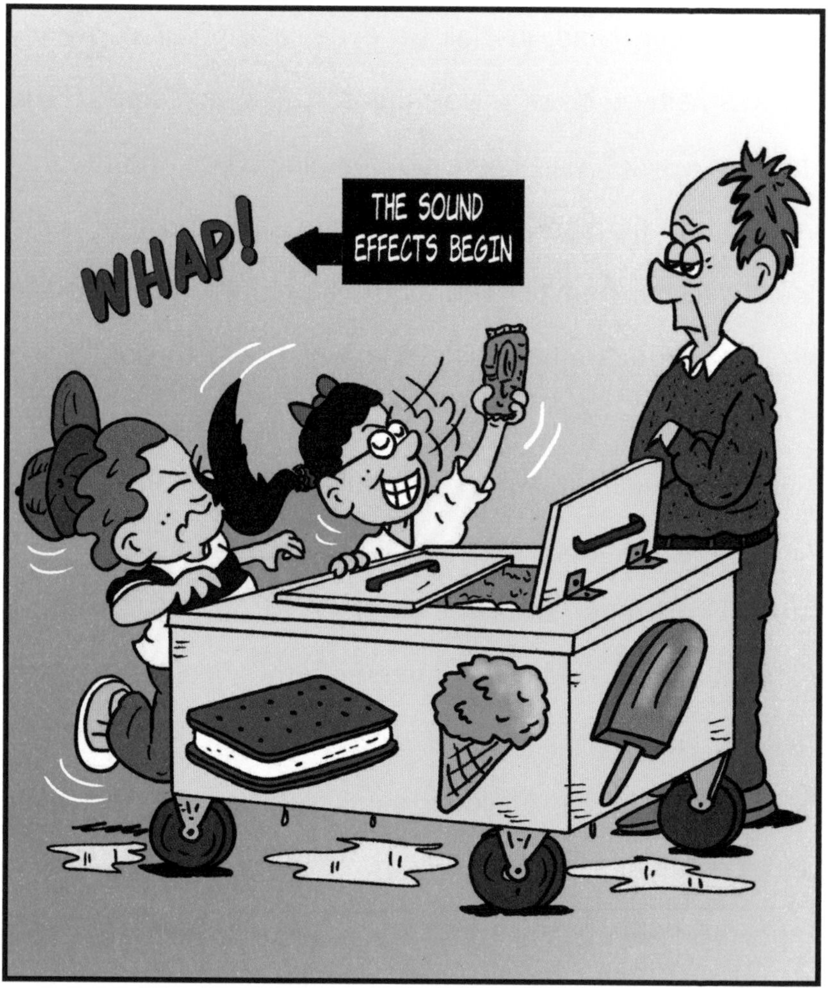
WHAP!
THE SOUND
EFFECTS BEGIN

"YES! FUDGESICLE!"

I grabbed it, handed over my fifty cents, and bounded back outside. I was grinning from ear to ear, but I tried not to show off. In my triumph, I wanted to be a better person than Wendy C., and I remembered what my parents always said: "Be a good winner."

"HA HA, SUCKERS! I GOT THE LAST FUDGESICLE, NOT WENDY!" I yelled. Nothing mean about that. Just stating the facts . . . loudly. I, ripped open the wrapper and chomped into that bad boy.

Pure deliciousness!

I chomped down again . . . even more deliciousness, plus a throat chill. I knew I should slow down, but I couldn't. The excitement of finding that last fudgesicle had taken over. Besides, I'm nine and a half years old, for crying out loud! I'm *supposed* to eat ice cream like a maniac! It's in the job description. I bit into my fudgesicle one more time and there it was . . .

BRAIN FREEZE! AAUUGGHH!

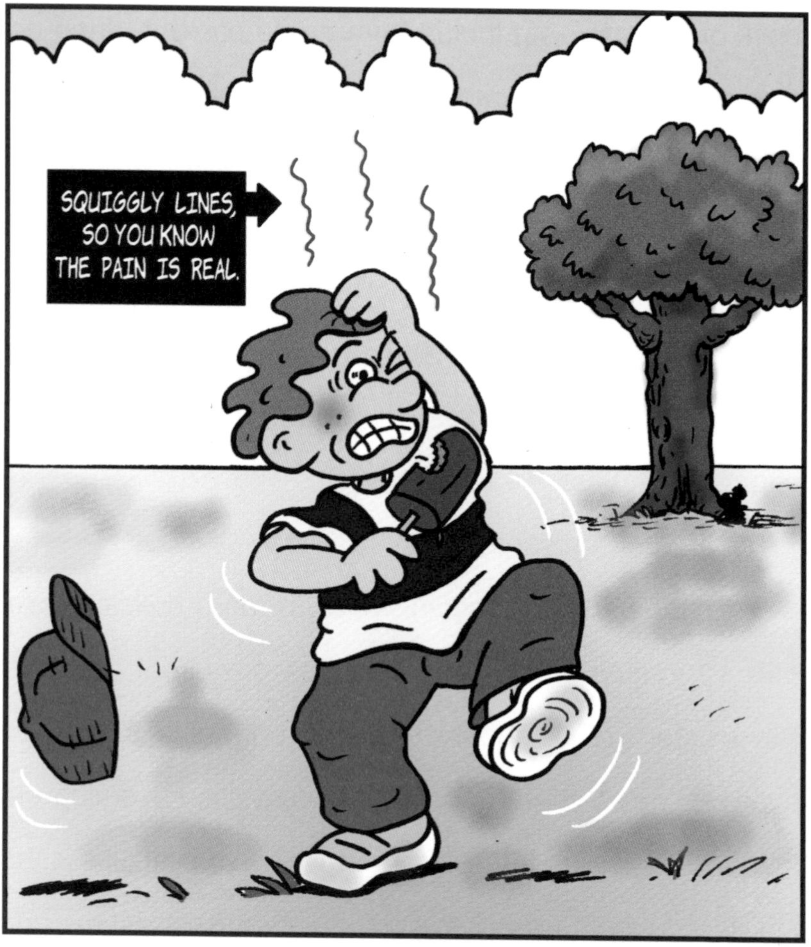
SQUIGGLY LINES, SO YOU KNOW THE PAIN IS REAL.

I'd had brain freeze before, lots of times. (We've already established I eat ice cream like a total pig.) That was my thing. But this time something was different. I started shaking, things got a little blurry. My hair tingled. Yes, my *hair* tingled. My whole body felt, um, energized—electric or something. Probably how Frankenstein's monster felt after that first jolt! Or Benjamin Franklin when his kite got zapped!

I felt like I didn't have control of myself anymore. My legs started vibrating, and ZOOM! Suddenly I took off with blazing speed toward the oak tree at the edge of the playground! I made it there in what seemed like one, maybe two seconds. I'll bet I was leaving one of those cartoon blurs behind me. When I got to the tree, I zipped halfway up the trunk, did a backflip, and landed right on my feet, as if I'd done it a hundred times.

WHOA!

Trembling, I looked down at my fudgesicle. What the heck is in this thing?! I wasn't sure whether I should throw it as far as I could or take another bite.

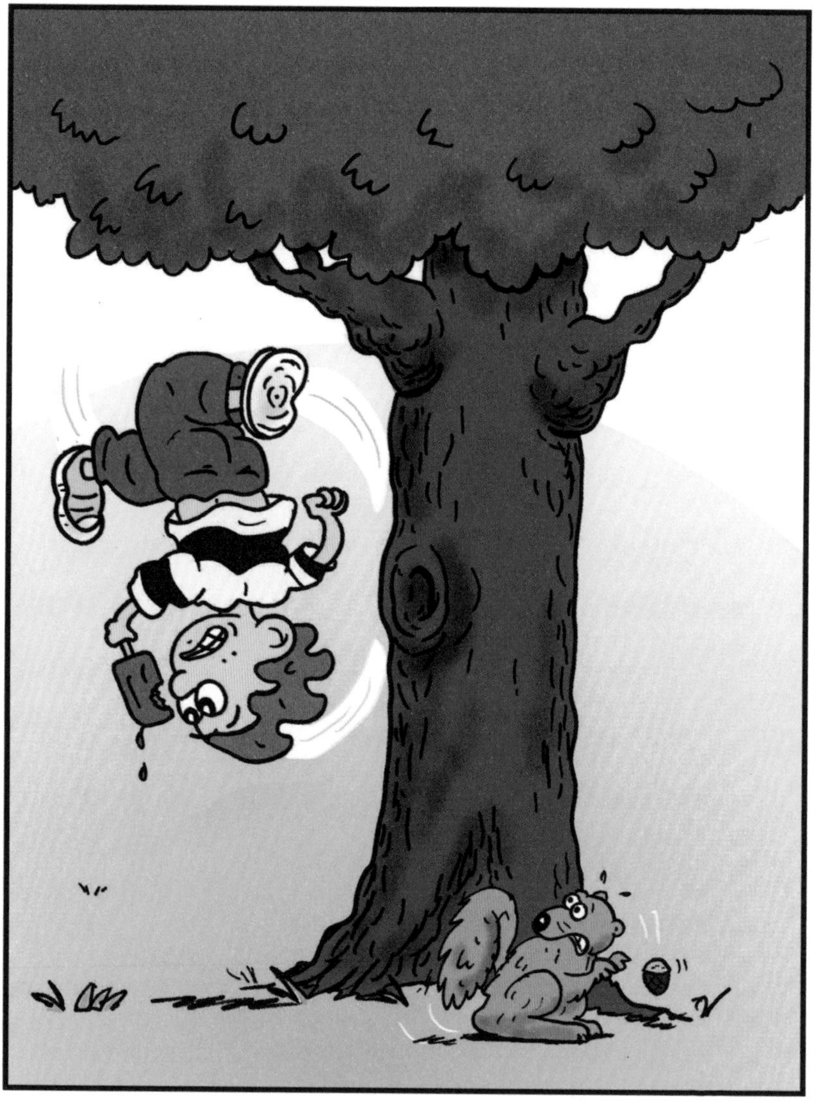

Being a pigboy, I took another bite . . .

and another brain freeze hit me!

I got that weird feeling again and did the zoom/climb/ flip thing, but this time I looked up when I heard "That back-flip was pretty sweet, dude."

A squirrel looked me right in the eyes; I stared back. Then it struck me.

A . . . squirrel . . . just . . . talked . . . to . . . me.

I fainted, face-first in the dirt.

When I woke up, the supersized face of Ms. Scabs, the school nurse, hovered over me, close enough for me to smell the tacos she had for lunch. I was dazed, confused, and had several questions.

"Am I okay?"

"What happened?"

"Did anyone save my fudgesicle?"

Ms. Scabs put a cold washcloth on my forehead and told me to lie back down.

Within a couple minutes, my mother had arrived at

school. Apparently it's school policy that if you faint face-first in the dirt, you're excused for the rest of the day.

The whole ride home Mom asked me over and over if I was okay, and about what had happened on the playground. I mostly just groaned that I was fine. I felt a little sick, and was starting to worry about how the guys were going to torture me endlessly for fainting. I'd have to come up with something. Maybe I could just say Mr. NO RUNNING! was a kid-hating ninja spy and had poisoned me! Yeah, that could happen. Well, at least the race was off for today.

The other reason I was worried was that I really didn't want to discuss what had happened. I mean, how do you tell somebody, "Oh, by the way, now I can run a hundred miles an hour, do tree flips, and talk to squirrels." It's kind of hard to just slip that into conversation without drawing some attention . . . or a well-deserved wedgie. Mom already said my imagination worked overtime. She'd never believe *anything* I said again if I told her that. Still, she looked worried. Almost like she knew something but wasn't telling.

Like that look a doctor would have right before saying, "Oh, and don't be surprised if your butt falls off later today."

"Butt" . . . now that's a funny word. Classic.

We turned onto Diamond Street, and I saw our house. I also saw Grandpa Gus's car parked out front.

"Cool," I said. "Grandpa's here."

"I told your grandfather what happened and he wanted to be here," Mom explained.

I loved my Grandpa Gus. He was a funny, odd old dude who always had a joke for me. Some of them I even understood. My friends thought Grandpa Gus looked older than most grandparents. Like maybe he'd lived a really hard life. Who knows? I just know he's cool. Maybe I could tell Grandpa about what happened.

CHAPTER 4

IN THE GENES

My mother insisted that I go lie down and rest. I talked her into just a couple minutes with Grandpa. I walked into the living room, and there was Gramps, on the recliner, reclined, and snoring . . . loudly.

I cleared my throat. "Auuh-Ughh."

Nothing.

Grandpa Gus was out like a rock. Well, you know, if rocks wore plaid shirts and black knee-high socks. Sleeping on the floor next to him was Captain, Grandpa's corgi that had to be at least 207 years old in dog time. Heck, maybe in people time. Captain farted. A lot. And I could swear that goofy-looking little dog smiled when he did it. Like he

knew the pain and suffering he was about to bring to others. I respected that about him. I'd kill to be able to toot on command.

I dropped my backpack on the floor hard.

THUD!

Captain barked loudly, waking up Gramps. Mission accomplished.

"Hey, Sport!" Grandpa Gus cried out.

"Hey, Gramps," I replied.

"Heard you had a little trouble at school today. You all right?" Grandpa Gus asked. I thought I detected a little smile on his face when he asked that. Weird. I decided to just blurt it out quickly all at once, like ripping off a Band-Aid! (Although, truth is, I still had my mom remove my frequent Band-Aids.)

Whew. Deep breath. Here goes . . .

"Grandpa Gus, today I bit into a fudgesicle, got lightning speed, did a backflip off a tree, and had a squirrel tell me it was cool!" I blurted out in less than two seconds. After I said it out loud for the first time, it didn't sound so strange.

Grandpa Gus remained silent, just staring at me as if I had two noses or something. (I checked my face real quick to see if I had grown another nose. Who knew what else could happen at this point?)

Grandpa rubbed his chin and said, "I see. I see. Well, I only have one thing to say to that, young man."

I waited for him to tell me to go lie down, that I was probably still confused from my smackdown with the dirt, but instead, Grandpa Gus stood up, smiled, and screamed, "YES! YES!"

FLYING TOOT. DON'T TRY THIS AT HOME...OR ANYWHERE.

Then he started dancing around in a circle, jumping up and down, knees and hips popping and snapping. This set Captain barking. I didn't know what to think of Grandpa's joy about me being a freak.

"EVELYN! GET IN HERE!" Grandpa cried out.

Mom came running in.

"WHAT?!" she yelled in a panic, spilling something from a mixing bowl all over the floor.

"Irwin's got it!" said Grandpa Gus. "He's got it! I told you it just skipped a generation!"

"Great," mumbled Mom.

"What I have I got?" I asked.

The two of them proceeded to discuss whether or not I had a certain "something." They talked like I wasn't standing *right there*.

"EXCUSE ME!!! Third person in the room here."

Grandpa looked at Mom. Mom sighed.

"Go ahead. Tell him," she said.

Gramps pulled me up on his lap, which we both

realized quickly was WAY too awkward. I stood by the recliner instead. He said he had a deep, dark secret to let me in on.

"Oh, Grandpa, we all know it's Captain that does the farting. It's no secret." I assured him. Captain shot me an evil grin.

Grandpa shook his head and patted my hand. "Irwin," he said, "you are part of a very special family . . . a family with very special powers . . ."

I waited for the punch line.

And waited . . .

and wondered how long I'd be waiting . . .

Neither Gramps nor Mom was smiling or laughing. Didn't seem like there was a joke coming. They just looked at me.

"Have you heard of Mighty Super Gus, Sport?" Gramps asked.

"Sure," I replied. "He fights crime all over Mock City. He's our hometown hero. Mighty Super Gus rules."

Grandpa slowly unbuttoned his flannel shirt. There was something shiny underneath . . . a spandex uniform . . . *with the famous MSG logo on it!*

"NO WAY!" I gasped.

"Way," answered Mom.

I stood there with my little mouth wide open; for a second, I felt like I might faint again. My whole world was completely changed. Then a thought hit me.

"So, is Dad a crime-fighting superhero, too?" I asked.

"Irwin, do you know about genes and what they contain?" Gramps asked.

"Mine usually contain dirt, and sometimes that white linty stuff," I said.

"Not the jeans you wear, the genes that make up your body. It's what's inside of YOU. And our family genes have SUPERHERO in them."

"So, is Dad a superhero or not?" Man, I was getting confused.

"No. At least not that we know about," Gramps replied. "Your dad got the accounting gene. It's not as exciting, but it pays the bills. The superhero gene must have skipped him and went on to you."

Mom just stood there looking worried the whole time, and then she walked away. And then something struck me . . . Mighty Super Gus had a crime-fighting sidekick . . . Captain Corgi. Whoa! All this time that barking little pointy-eared tooter was a superhero. Captain farted. But this time it sounded more heroic to me.

"Congratulations, Irwin, you're going to be the next crime-fighting SUPERHERO in the family!" Grandpa beamed.

I hope this doesn't mean I have to eat extra vegetables or anything.

CHAPTER 5

COOKIES AND CATS

Grandpa was incredibly excited about all this. "Let's get you training right away!" he said.

Mom heard that from the other room. She was next to us immediately.

"Gus, he's been through enough for one day. Irwin, I want you to go lie down for a little bit."

That didn't seem right, so I questioned her.

"Are you allowed to make superheroes take a nap?"

The look she gave me said "yes."

Mom left, and I started toward my room. Grandpa grabbed my arm, pulled me close, and whispered, "Meet me out back in ten minutes." He winked at me, and I knew what his plan was. Sneak out the window in my room.

I went upstairs and tossed my backpack carefully into a pile of clothes. I was trying to decide if I should change into shorts when I heard the thump against the house. It was Grandpa Gus with the ladder. We'd done this before a couple of times. I crawl out my window, and then Grandpa and I would go do something. It's always fun, risky, kind of scary, and totally wrong. I usually feel guilty while I'm doing it. Kids, don't try this at home. That's my first bit of superhero advice.

I could see the top of the ladder and Grandpa's smiling, eager face over the edge of the roof. He was holding up a fudgesicle.

"Yes!" I said.

I had one leg out the window when Mom knocked on the door. AAUUGGHH! Busted. I jumped to my bed and pretended to be resting.

"Irwin, you've got company." Mom came in the room with Trey and Elisha right behind her.

"HOMEWORK!" said Elisha, way too excitedly.

"Why is your window open?" asked Mom.

"Um, I, um, thought some fresh air might do me some good."

Quick thinking. Just like a superhero.

"Plus, this room smells like the sewer pond by the edge of town," added Elisha. "It needs airing out."

As Trey settled into a video game on my computer, Elisha stood near my bed and explained the homework. She stood a little too close. There was a rumor at school that Elisha had a crush on me. AAUUGGHH! A crush is when a girl likes a boy, and wants to "crush" his ability to play with his friends. At least that's MY understanding of it.

It was a light load of homework for Ms. Frost: six pages of math, five pages of sentence diagramming, and a three-fourths-scale model of the Sphinx to be built out of empty milk cartons.

"Um, okay, I guess you guys better get going," I said. I was anxious to get to the ice cream.

"Not yet, dude. I'm getting my best score ever here," said Trey.

Meanwhile, Elisha was telling a story about something that happened in P.E., I wasn't really paying attention, and she could tell.

"Irwin! Are you listening to me?"

"Yeah. Totally. Great story."

"So you think it's cool that Mikey Wolfer shoved an entire tennis ball in his nostril?" she asked.

I thought about it a second.

"Actually, yes."

Trey finally lost the game, and they got up to leave. He punched me in the arm on the way out. "That's for fainting, you wuss."

I deserved that.

I started back out the window when there was another knock. Oh, c'mon! It was my sweet Grandma Joyce. She had a plate of her homemade cookies. NOOOOOO! I had the only grandma on earth who couldn't cook. Her baked goods were the worst. She sat down next to me.

"Brought you some treats, Irwin."

"Gee, thanks, Grandma."

"I heard about what happened and want you to know everything will be just fine."

She hugged me tight. One of the curlers in her hair poked me in the eye, but she made me feel good. That's what grandmas do.

"Now, you eat up all these cookies."

"I, uh, should probably save them for dessert," I said, thinking quickly.

"Nonsense. After a day like today, you deserve them now. Promise me you'll clean your plate."

"I promise."

Grandma Joyce left, and I went back to the window. Grandpa stuck his head back up.

"What's going on? When did you get so popular?" he asked.

"You need to help me eat these cookies before we can train," I said.

Grandpa Gus got a look of panic in his eyes. He'd been eating those cookies for, like, forty years. He crawled up on the roof and in my window. He grabbed a cookie and gave me a tip.

"Plug your nose, chew fast, and try and think of some other place you'd rather be."

We started in on them.

"Awww. This one tastes like shoelaces."

"Ewww. This one tastes like asparagus."

That went on for a couple minutes, but we finished the plate, as promised.

"Okay! It's showtime!" Gramps grinned.

We carefully crawled out the window and onto the small ledge of roof.

"Wait," I said. "Who's holding the ladder?"

"Captain is. Why?"

"How can a corgi hold a ladder? His legs are like half an inch long."

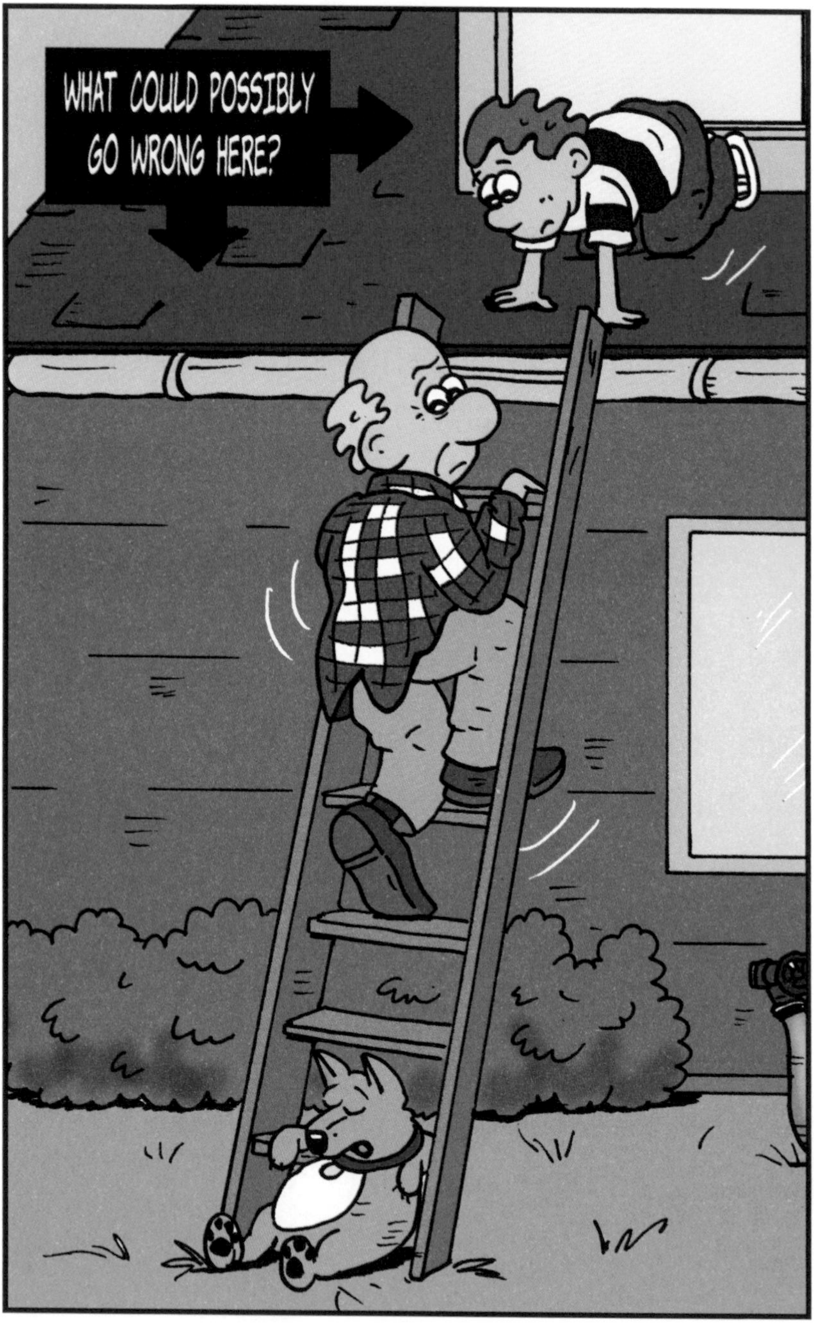
WHAT COULD POSSIBLY GO WRONG HERE?

Grandpa went down first and then held the ladder for me. He pulled the fudgesicle from his shirt pocket.

"Now, let's see what this baby can do!" He grinned.

Just then we heard Mom singing over on the side of the house! If she was singing, it meant she was watering her flowers. She's coming this way!

"Head for the bushes!" whispered Grandpa.

We ran across the yard and dove into them. Even Captain did! I think that little dog was actually having fun. He seemed to know we were in danger. Then he farted. Our perfect hiding place now smelled like skunk bottom.

Mom was whistling and singing and watering her flowers.

"We're safe here," whispered Grandpa. Then something brushed against my leg. I looked down and tried my hardest not to scream. Right there in the bushes with us was the meanest, most nasty creature on the planet.

Mr. Fluffers, our neighbors' cat.

This thing was the size of a Volkswagen, and pure evil.

It hissed and bared its yellow, pointy teeth at us. Captain Corgi couldn't take it. I don't blame him. He bolted from the bushes, yelping in a very high dog voice. If Mom weren't twenty feet away I'd have done the same thing.

"Grandpa, I'm scared," I whispered.

"Me, too, Irwin. Me, too," he said. Mr. Fluffers kept staring at us with those green eyes, and then turned his back to us.

"Maybe he's leaving," I said hopefully.

"Nope," said Grandpa. "He's peeing."

"AAAUUUGGGHHH!" We both screamed as we ran from the bushes. We nearly smacked into Mom, who turned the hose on us out of fright.

Then she just looked at us with that disappointed look that always makes me feel terrible.

"Your father will be home in a minute for dinner. Go wash up."

We walked away in shame. Then Mom added, "And you're both grounded."

Wow, mom power is way stronger than superhero power.

CHAPTER 6

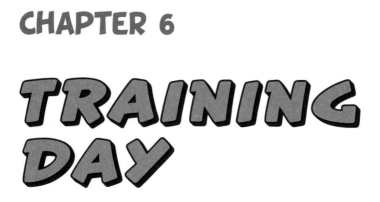

I woke up Saturday morning feeling pretty darned good. Hey, maybe this superhero stuff could be pretty cool. I mean, who knows what powers I might have? Maybe I can fly? That would be awesome, cruising along through the air, high-fiving Superman. Anyhow, first things first, and that means a game of baseball with the guys in the park. I grabbed my favorite stinky ball cap and headed downstairs. Grandpa Gus was waiting in the kitchen with a cooler full of frozen treats. Shoot. Baseball would have to wait.

"TRAINING DAY!" Gramps shouted.

Dad read the newspaper. He didn't look happy. He gave me a hug and told me this was all my decision. Mom

agreed. Wow! That never happened. Nothing was ever *MY*
decision. Chalk one up in the superhero-plus column.

They said if I just wanted to play with my friends and be

a fourth grader that it was perfectly fine with them. Grandpa winked at me and whispered, "Boooorrrring."

"Dad, what's the rush to start his training?" my father asked Grandpa Gus. "My goodness, we just found out about this yesterday!"

"There's talk amongst the superheroes about possible trouble," Gramps replied. "Something to do with the recent rash of robberies around town."

I sat at the table not knowing what to do. I know most people would think "What kid wouldn't want to be a superhero?" It seems like a no-brainer. (Did I use that term correctly?)

But Grandpa was already talking about fighting crime. I hadn't even had my training yet. That was a little scary. Was superhero really the right career choice for me? These days I was leaning more toward zombie-baseball-playing surfer. Seemed a lot more realistic than superhero.

Mom set a plate of scrambled eggs, bacon, and jelly toast down in front of me.

"NONSENSE!" yelled Grandpa. "That's not going to do us any good."

He grabbed the plate and set it on the table for Captain. The old dog farted and wagged his little stub of a tail. Then he inhaled the food. Grandpa set *another* plate in front of me with a fudgesicle and a drumstick on it, and not the

chicken drumstick, the awesome ice cream kind.

"YES! Ice cream for breakfast! Just how nature intended it to be!" I squealed. Chalk up another one in the superhero, plus column.

Mom grabbed the plate right back and started making me another round of eggs. I sure hoped she was going to rinse off the corgi slobber first. She shot Grandpa Gus one of her *looks*, and he didn't argue. He slumped down in a chair and checked his phone for messages. He seemed concerned about what he was reading.

I *was* really just planning on meeting the guys for baseball in the park today. I'd recently mastered bike riding with no hands, and was sure I was ready to try it while juggling a mitt, hat, bat, water bottle, and baseball.

Grandpa returned to his training day plans. He started smiling again. I hadn't seen him this happy since he found out he could watch *Star Trek* online. This whole superhero thing did explain a couple things about Grandpa, like how

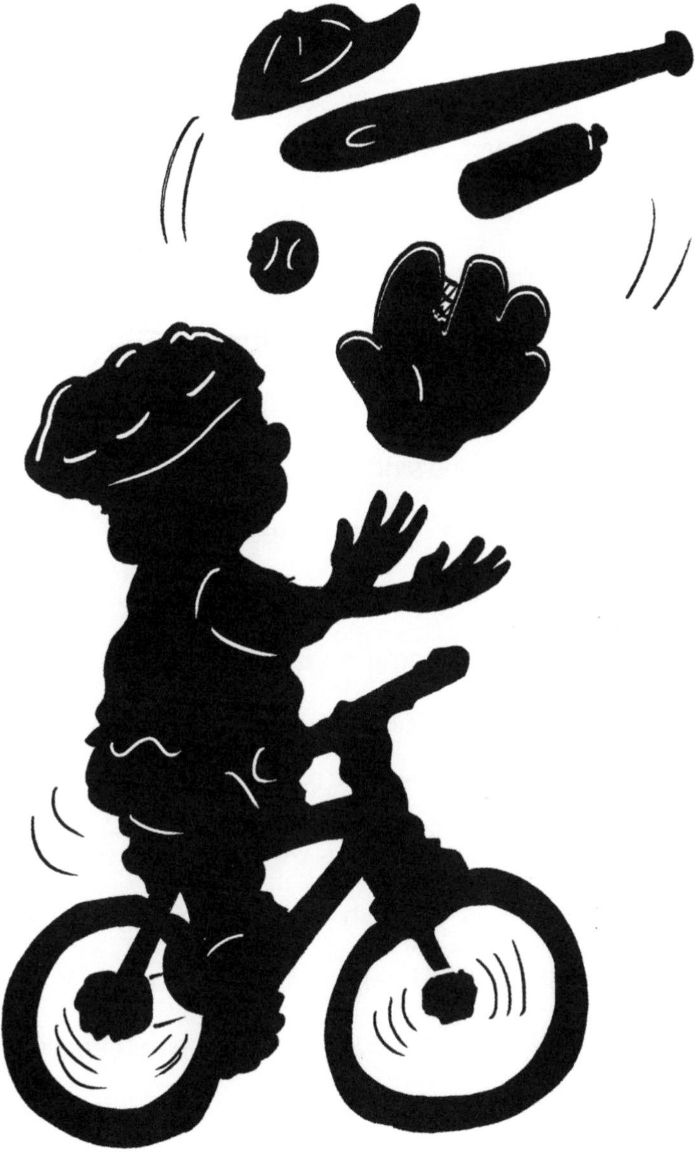

he was sore a lot and why he looked so old. Probably came from years of battling crime. This was something I'd need to think about. I mean, right now I don't really care about how I look, but I understand it's ALL you think about when you become a teenager.

I figured I could skip ONE Saturday of baseball. But I'm not gonna lie . . . I was getting worried about all of this stuff. Fighting criminals, missing ball games with my friends, and getting gray hair as a fourth grader.

Dad had a talk with Grandpa about how this training session was just "testing the waters." Whatever that means. Old people say a lot of things that make no sense—and most of them start like this: "When I was your age . . ."

Grandpa assured Dad we would take things slow and that there was no rush to hone my craft. That made no sense *and* sounded painful. What was my craft anyway? Probably something that grows on you when you get older, like ear hair. Well, nobody was honing it without getting a good fight from me.

Before we left, Mom and Dad had a talk with me about how I was special, even without the superhero stuff.

They also told me school came first, and that I needed to remember to just be a kid. Apparently they didn't realize as a fourth grader, I wasn't a kid anymore. I was a *dude*.

Grandpa and I left for training.

CHAPTER 7

DUCKS ARE JERKS

We drove to Off-Central Park, a massive place near the center of Mock City. It had everything: ponds, ballparks, a zoo, a place where bands played, and the best food vendor carts in the world. We went to the far end of the park, where it was usually pretty quiet, except for teenagers sometimes making out.

Gross.

As part of training, Grandpa had *me* carry the cooler of ice cream. I'm pretty sure that wasn't training, just Grandpa Gus getting out of work. We found the perfect spot. Well, actually it was the spot where I told Gramps, "I can't carry this stupid thing any farther!"

We decided to try and see if different ice creams would give me different powers. Grandpa reached in the cooler and grabbed an ice cream sandwich.

"Let's give this one a try."

"Those aren't really my favorites," I said.

"It's 9:00 in the morning, and I'm giving you ice cream."

He made a good point.

Grandpa told me, "Repeat exactly what happened on the playground . . . except for the booger contest." He grinned. "Just a little joke to break the tension."

I unwrapped the ice cream sandwich. I think there was a part of me that was kind of hoping nothing would happen. I could still catch the guys for baseball, and put all this stuff behind me. But, more importantly, I could just be a dude . . . not a superhero. Seemed like a *lot* of pressure would come with the hero thing.

I cautiously nibbled on the corner of the frozen treat.

Nothing.

"C'mon! No pain, no gain!" Grandpa smacked me on the back of the head.

I chomped down hard on a huge bite . . . and there it was . . . *the freeze.*

I got that tingly, energized feeling, but I didn't take off running. I looked at a plump pigeon that had hopped up on a nearby bench. Our eyes locked, like in a staring contest. It was odd. Kind of like this chubby pigeon could read my mind, like that thing Mr. Spock does. I was having a pigeon mind-meld.

"The little dog stinks. What on Earth do you guys feed him?" said the pigeon.

I was shocked. I mean, c'mon, talking to a *pigeon*? A squirrel was one thing, but a pigeon? That's just weird.

"Did you hear that?" I asked my grandpa.

All Gramps heard was that cooing sound pigeons make. But he could tell by the look on my face that something had happened. I chomped into the ice cream sandwich again. The brain freeze came easier this time. I looked at the chubby little bird and asked,

"What's your name?"

"You wouldn't be able to understand it," the pigeon responded rudely.

"Give me a try," I shot back.

The bird made those pigeony coo-coo sounds for several seconds and then stared at me.

"Could you translate that to people talk?" I asked.

"Bert," the bird replied.

"You're Bert the pigeon?" I asked.

"Are your ears plugged?"

Bert the pigeon appeared to have an attitude.

Captain Corgi gave Bert the pigeon a dirty look and growled. Maybe he understood him. Not sure. I didn't know WHAT to think at this point. I chomped into the sandwich one more time and got a slight freeze. I looked at Captain and asked, "Can you and I talk?"

Captain Corgi looked at me right in the eyes, and then

turned and licked himself in the doggie privates. I took that as a "No."

So Grandpa Gus wrote down in his training journal: *1. Ice cream sandwich = talk to animals.* At least rude pigeons.

"Let's try another kind of ice cream," Gramps suggested.

"Don't have to ask me twice!" I said.

Just then Gramps's phone rang. I never noticed before what a cool phone he had. He mostly listened and nodded and said things like, "I understand."

"Everything okay?" I asked. "We still eating ice cream?"

"Yeah, um, we just need to hurry it along for now," Gramps replied. "We're not going to figure out all your powers in one morning, anyhow."

Grandpa Gus said it might take years to train and get my superhero stuff down, and that we could work as a team until I was ready to take over the family business. He was "easing" into retirement. Mostly because he said he still sucked at golf, and hated bingo. Still, the thought of taking over the superhero business concerned me. It meant my whole life was already planned out for me. I mean, once the city is counting on you to save them, you're stuck, right? You can't just say, "Um, think I'm going bowling now. You guys are on your own." Mighty Super Gus had been saving Mock City forever, and he always came through. This city definitely needed a hero. It was one strange thing after another in this town. Was I up for that challenge?

I was planning on being a kid until the Zit Fairy came along. I figured that was the end of your good years. Then I'd give in to the whole boyfriend/girlfriend thing. After all, I'd have nothing else to live for. Of course, *now* I might be able to just ZAP the Zit Fairy into oblivion with some cool power. (Not sure where oblivion is. I think it's near Boise.)

Grandpa pulled out a fudgesicle.

"All right!" I said. "Party time!"

Bert the pigeon hopped on the top of the bench for a better view. I got nervous all over again. Grandpa told me to try and focus my energy. I bit down hard on a big bite, in my typical piglike fashion. I started to shake. I felt all tingly. I looked at Bert.

"You gonna puke? Cause I can't handle puke," said the bird. He sounded sort of disgusted.

I was vibrating, and couldn't control myself any longer.

"Aim for the pond!" Gramps yelled, just as I started taking off at top speed! I got to the pond in like, two seconds . . . only I couldn't stop! I ran right across the top of the water, straight through a flock of ducks! This was crazy! It was the coolest and scariest thing ever at the same time!

The ducks scattered as fast as they could. One of them screamed, "Hey, you kid, get off our lawn! I mean pond!"

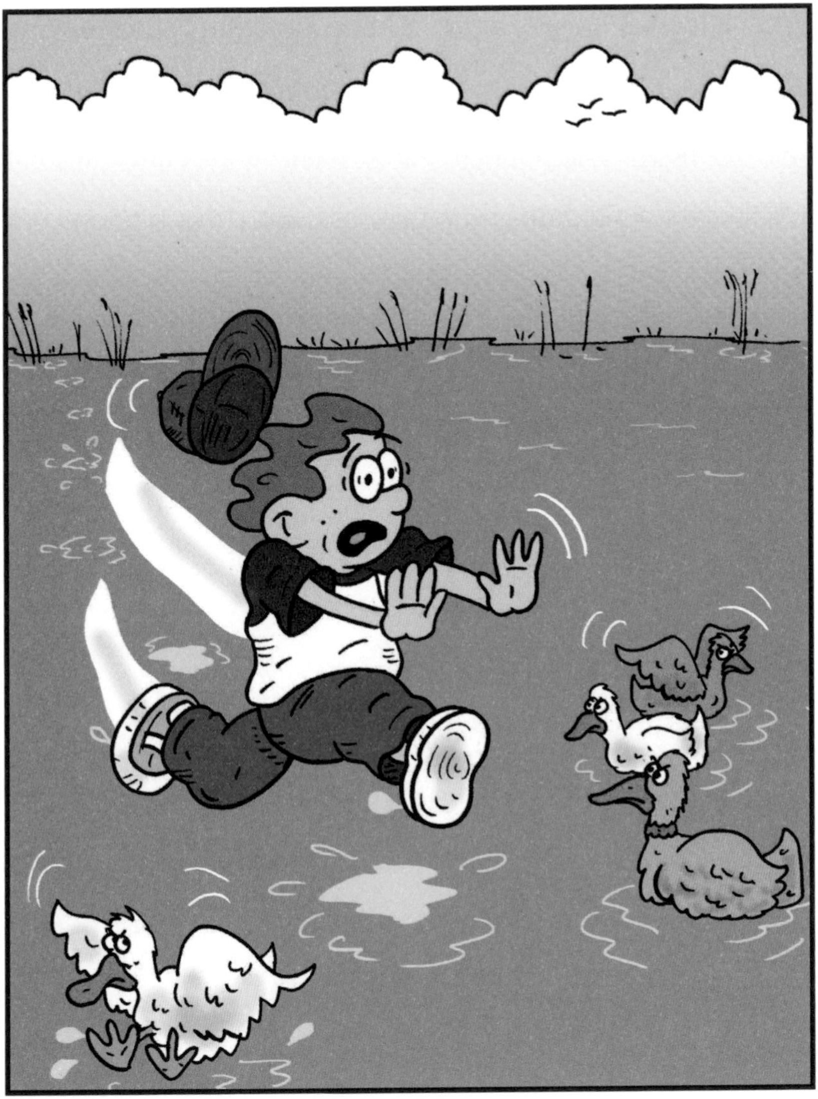

I was still going at top speed, and starting to freak out! What if I never slowed down?! In desperation I stuck out my arm and tried to grab a small tree. I held on just long enough to spin halfway around the tree trunk and launch myself back toward Grandpa, Captain, and Bert the pigeon! But the pond was in my way again. I started right back across it. This time one of the ducks stuck out a little webbed foot and tripped me, totally on purpose! That was no accident.

"NOT COOL!" I screamed.

I slid across the water on my stomach and face and ended up on the edge of some reeds . . . about an inch from a turtle's butt.

"May I help you?" the turtle asked in a rather snotty tone.

This was where my lifelong hatred of ducks came from. Grandpa was standing over me when I looked up. I couldn't tell if he was bursting with pride or about to laugh. Probably a little of both.

"You okay?" Gramps grinned.

I grunted.

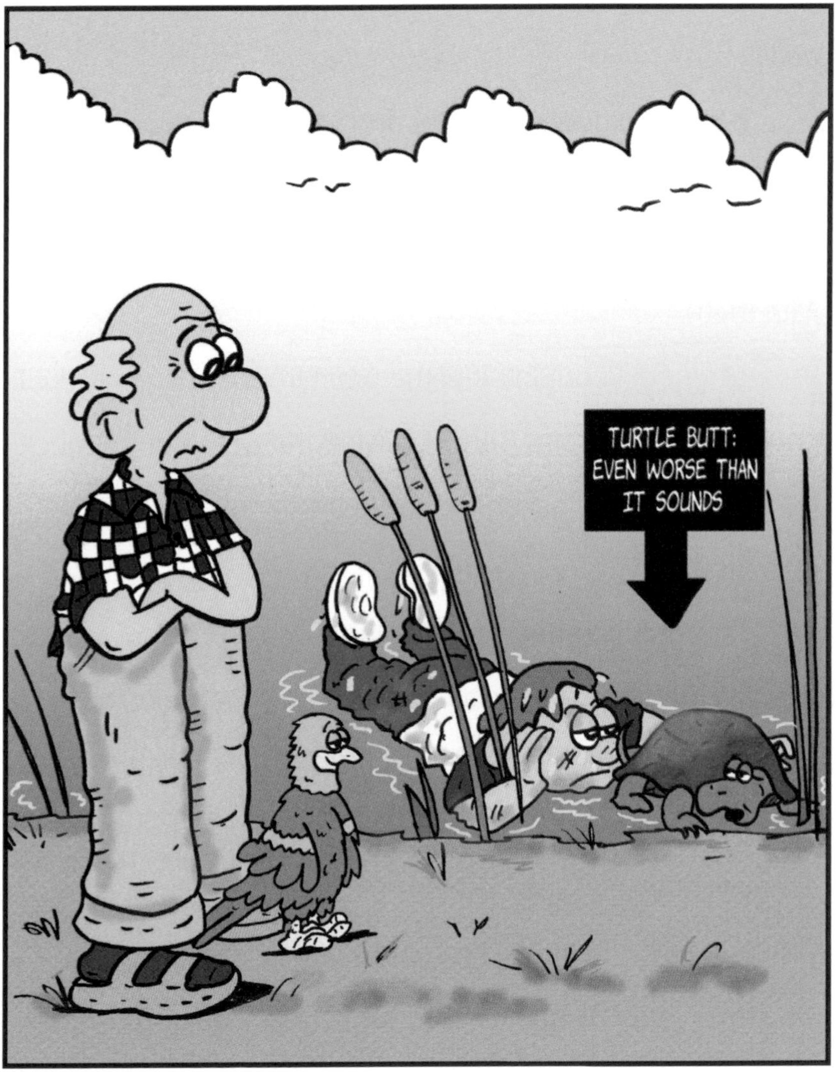
TURTLE BUTT:
EVEN WORSE THAN
IT SOUNDS

"That . . . was *amazing*," Grandpa Gus added. He jotted down: *2. fudgesicle = super speed and talking to animals ability.*

Bert the pigeon flew over and yelled, "Ducks are jerks!" He was talking to me, but said it loud enough for the ducks to hear, too. It was obvious this wasn't his first encounter with them.

Strange. I couldn't feel the brain freeze anymore, but I could still understand Bert. I crawled out of the pond muck, leaned down, and asked the turtle his name.

Nothing.

The turtle's mouth moved, but I couldn't connect with him. Maybe I had a special deal with Bert the pigeon.

Grandpa decided (and I agreed) that it was probably enough training for the first time out. He was in a bit of a hurry now as well. "No need to rush training things," Grandpa said. "Besides, I've got to get."

We gathered up our stuff and started back to the car. Neither of us picked up the cooler.

"You're still in training," said Gramps. He turned and started walking.

I sighed and picked up the cooler. Bert the pigeon landed on top of it.

"Another pound or two isn't going to matter. Forward!"

On the trip back to the parking lot, I asked Grandpa a few things.

"When did you learn about your powers?"

"I was fourteen years old. I tried something called Beech-Nut Gum. Ever heard of it?"

"Nope."

"I started chewing on that gum and got that tingle."

"Yeah! It's kind of a tingle," I said.

"Only I'm lucky enough to not get brain freezes with mine," he added. "I ran like I'd never run before. Kind of scared me, to be honest."

"Mighty Super Gus gets scared?" I asked

"I wasn't always Mighty Super Gus. I was a kid just like you once, buddy. But I slowly got control of my speed and superstrength. And trust me, that first time you help someone, or save the city, it gets you hooked."

Gramps put his arm around me. I felt a little better about all this.

He started telling me about some of his battles back in the day with some of Mock City's greatest villains, like The Prankster, and The Flamingo, and The Green Apple. I remember hearing about some of those bad guys. Weird to think it was MY grandpa who had saved our old town so many times. The more detail he went into about them, the more these villains sounded like the kind you'd find in a book or a movie . . . or a book that was made into a movie.

By the time we made it to the car, my arms were killing me. Bert the pigeon hopped down off the cooler and cried, "SHOTGUN!"

"No way is a filthy pigeon riding in the front seat of my car," said Gramps. "It's a classic. Like me."

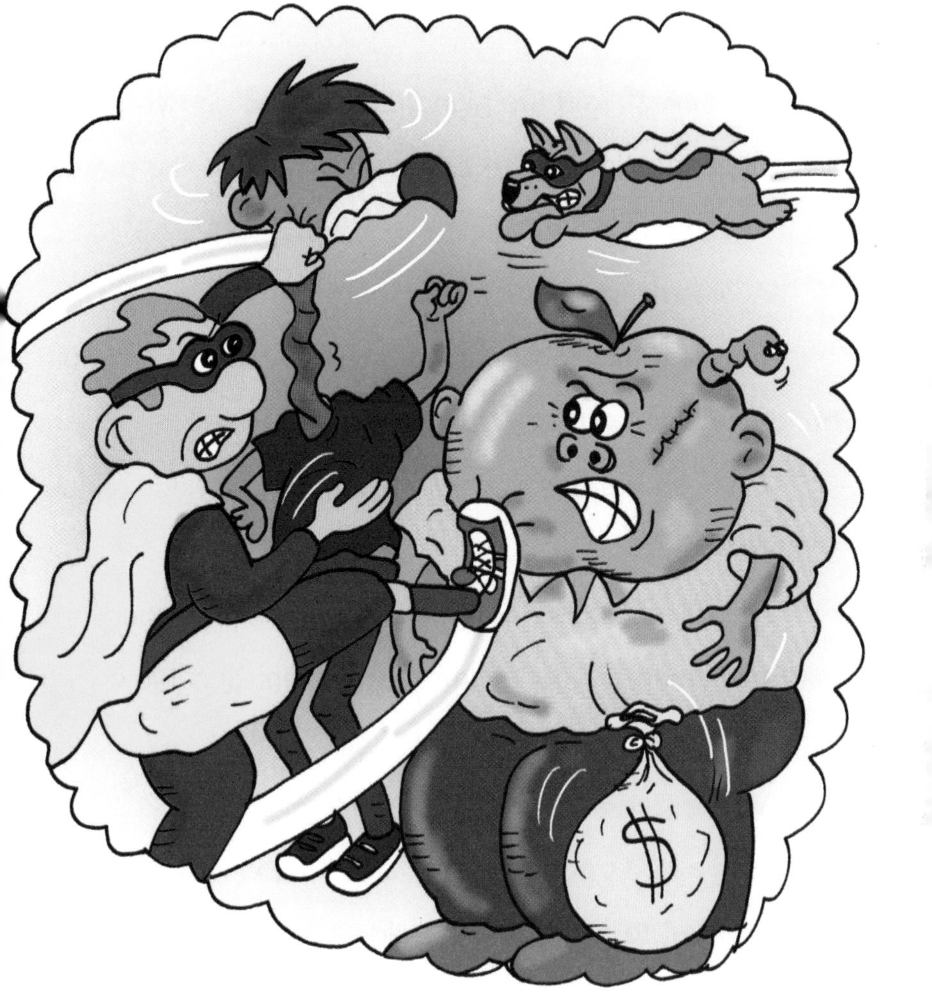

"Help me out, Irving," said Bert.

"Irwin," I corrected.

"Whatever," said the pigeon. "Look, me and you got a special connection. We're a team, Erskin. Just like the old dude and the dog that smells like rotten eggs."

"Again, my name is Irwin," I said.

"I need to go home with you. There's an unbreakable bond between us. I can feel it," Bert said.

"I'm not sure. This is all happening so fast. I don't know what to think."

Then Bert added, "Maybe this will help. If you don't take me along, I'll go to the newspapers and blow your superhero identities."

"You're starting a relationship with blackmail?" I asked.

"Hey, a bird's gotta do what a bird's gotta do."

I turned to Gramps and said, "Looks like the bird is coming with us."

"Well, I guess Harry Potter's got his majestic snowy owl . . . and Irwin, you've got this flying rat from the park."

Grandpa also said Bert *still* wasn't riding in the car.

So we drove home with an infuriated pigeon clinging to the car's antenna—and I finally got to hear all those words they bleep out on TV.

CHAPTER 8

EATEN BY BADGERS

When we pulled up in the driveway, I realized I'd have to explain Bert the pigeon to Mom and Dad.

They weren't going to like this one bit.

Dad's a bit of a neat freak. Okay, he's a full-blown cleanaholic. And Mom hadn't allowed me to have any new pets since the "ant farm incident." She didn't care much for the farting corgi that visited now and then. I can't imagine her reaction to a pigeon that's probably not potty-trained.

We walked up to the front door (actually, Bert *flew* up).

"Be cool and calm," I told the pigeon. "Don't ruffle any feathers."

Get it? Ruffle any feathers? 'Cause he's a bird?

Bert and Grandpa didn't laugh, either. Bert the pigeon agreed to be mellow.

"Not a peep out of me," Bert promised.

"Not a poop would be nice as well," I added.

Gramps, Bert, and I entered the house—and my worst nightmare came true. Bert absolutely flipped out!

"WHOA! NICE PLACE! XBOX 360! I'M HOME, BABY! I'M HOME!" he screeched, as he flew around the house.

"DO YOU HAVE A POOL? A TRAMPOLINE? IS THAT CAP'N CRUNCH ON THE COUNTER? YES! SCORE!"

Of course, to everyone but me, Bert sounded like a pigeon stuck in a lawn mower. He jumped on the kitchen table and started pecking at the butter. Mom screamed. Dad screamed louder. I got Bert down and tried to start this all over.

"Mom, Dad, this is Bert the pigeon," I said calmly.

"Pleasure to meet you," said Bert.

"They can't understand you," I explained to Bert.

Dad's mouth dropped open.

"Irwin, son, are you talking to a pigeon?"

"Yeah. Something wrong with that?"

Dad looked over at Gramps.

"What on Earth did you do to our boy, Pops?!"

"Dad, it's one of my powers. I can talk to animals after eating ice cream sandwiches. And Bert and I have a special connection. He's going to be my sidekick . . . if I decide to do this whole superhero thing."

I wasn't completely convinced yet this was the career path for me, especially after coming so close to a turtle's butt. That seemed very "unsuperheroish" . . . I just made that word up.

After getting Bert mostly under control and calming down my parents, we all came up with a plan. Bert could live on my window ledge . . . *outside*. But only if I potty-trained him, because apparently pigeons just poop wherever they are . . . kind of like toddlers. Bert didn't care for this plan one little bit.

"Superheros don't live on ledges!" he insisted. "They throw villains off of them!"

I reminded the pigeon that technically he was a sidekick . . . *maybe*. It all depended on what I decided to do. But Bert kept ranting about it.

"Would Batman make Robin live on a ledge? What about the Green Hornet? Would he shove Toto out on a ledge?!"

"Kato," I corrected.

I told Bert we'd figure it out later. I was exhausted from superhero training. I just wanted to rest—and get the image of that turtle's hiney out of my head.

I woke up to Trey tapping my forehead.

"Wake up, Sleeping *Ugly*," he laughed.

I looked at the clock. It was after 1:00 in the afternoon! I'd slept for a couple of hours! On a Saturday, a *nonschool* day! I wasn't going to do this superhero thing if it was going to cut into my leisure time so much.

Just as I swung up out of bed, Trey saw Bert the pigeon on the ledge.

"Duuuuuude! You've got one mad-looking pigeon on your window ledge. Hey! It's a real-life angry bird!"

Bert saw that I was awake and started yelling at me again.

"Would the Lone Ranger stick Toronto out on a ledge?!"

"Tonto," I mumbled under my breath.

I realized Trey was hearing him, too.

"Did you hear that?" I asked cautiously.

"Yeah," Trey answered.

"And you understood him?"

"Yeah, of course. He said "pigeon talk pigeon talk pigeon talk." What's wrong with you, Irwin? Did that fainting do something to your brain, dude?" Trey asked.

"Uh, I'm just messin' with you," I answered. "I'll meet you downstairs."

Bert knocked on the window.

"Hey! Am I coming with you?"

"No. This is playtime, not superhero stuff," I said.

"Then let me inside. I'll just hang out," said Bert.

"I can't. You're not allowed. Remember? You live on the ledge."

"Let me inside or I'll fly over the top of you dropping pigeon bombs. If you know what I mean," Bert said.

So with Bert the pigeon tucked comfortably in my bed, watching stuff on YouTube, I took off with Trey to ride bikes. We decided to ride up Dravis Street. It was the steepest street around, which meant it was perfect for coasting down at dangerously high speeds. Dravis Street had produced some of the greatest broken bones in Mock City history.

We huffed and puffed our way to the top. The nap must have done me some good, 'cause I felt great. It was the first time I'd ever beaten Trey to the top. We caught our breath, counted to three, and took off screaming, in a tough-guy way, downhill at what was probably two or three hundred miles an hour. That's just a guess, but probably pretty close.

Halfway down, I opened my eyes for a second. Odd, because I rarely do that. I spotted Grandpa Gus waiting for us at the bottom of the hill. What's this? I thought superhero training was over for the day. This is *kid time*! This stunk because the whole point of riding down Dravis Street was to coast as far as you, but could now I was going to have to stop my ridiculously dangerous momentum. Jimmy Trowbridge swore he once coasted all the way to Hollywood, where he ended up having to fight the creepy monkey from *Dora the Explorer* over a half a slice of pepperoni pizza that was lying in the street. I'm not convinced that entire story is true. I mean, c'mon, don't monkeys just eat bananas?

I screeched to a stop and asked Grandpa, "What's up?"

Grandpa whispered in my ear, "Trouble across town. BIG trouble. We need to go."

"Trey, I'm afraid I need to take Irwin. There's a family emergency!"

"What is it?" Trey asked. "Can I help?"

"Irwin's mother is being eaten by a badger!" Gramps blurted out.

"And you took the time to come get Irwin?" asked Trey.

He had a point.

I waited for Gramps's answer.

Silence.

Then I realized Grandpa Gus was just lying! (Are superheroes allowed to do that?) For some reason, he wanted to get me out of there. Gramps snatched my bike, put it in the trunk, and hustled me into his car. Trey waved good-bye as we sped off.

I gotta admit, I was a little mad here. This was MY time, and besides, I still wasn't sure I *wanted* to be in the superhero business. So far all it had done was make me sleepy and land me WAY too close to a turtle's butt. (Last time I'll mention that, I promise.)

Grandpa explained the crisis as he drove.

CHAPTER 9

PUT YOUR TIGHTS ON

"Irwin, Sweaty Crocker has broken out of prison. She's on the loose!"

"Seems like someone is ALWAYS breaking out of Mock City's prison," I said.

"It's the low budget they have. Hard to control prisoners when all you have to stop them with is water balloons," said Grandpa.

"So, who IS this person?" I asked.

"Sweaty Crocker is a former lunch lady from YOUR school," Gramps explained. "She was fired when kids kept getting sick from her dreadful cooking. Kind of like your grandmother's stuff."

"What?!" I yelled. "The killer lunch lady really exists?"

Apparently Sweaty Crocker had never actually killed any children. But she sent an awful lot of them to the school nurse. She also had several health violations for mice in her hairnets and excessive toenails in the meatloaf. All things that normally would have gone overlooked, but Sweaty Crocker went too far: She nearly did wipe out four kids with her cooking. And our school district has a very strict "nearly kill three kids and you're out" policy. I guess they cut Sweaty Crocker a little slack since she hung around long enough to almost take out a fourth. They probably couldn't get a sub for her or something.

Anyhow, Sweaty was on the loose, looking for revenge and causing a lot of damage in the process. She was taking it out on the whole city; everybody was going to pay for the fact that she got fired. We had to act now.

But it was Saturday!

I had kind of been hoping to play with my friends. If crime that called for superheroes was going to happen on the weekends, that was gonna be a really big check in the negative column for me.

Once we got home, Grandpa told me to go up to my room for a surprise.

"But hurry up. You know, we gotta save the city and all."

"Uh, right," I answered.

First thing I saw (or should I say *heard*) when I got to my room was Bert the pigeon snoring soundly on my pillow. It also looked like he'd been snacking on the secret Butterfinger stash I kept in my nightstand.

Second thing I saw, lying right in the middle of my bed, was a little superhero outfit. I picked it up. The pigeon rustled.

"Keep it down!" Bert snapped. "If I don't have a four-hour nap every day, I get . . . unpleasant."

The uniform was blue, with orange letters across the front that spelled ICK.

"Ain't she a beauty?" Gramps yelled from the doorway. "You're the Ice Cream Kid! That's your superhero name!"

I held up the outfit and looked at it again.

"But it says 'ick'," I pointed out, thinking maybe Gramps hadn't caught that the first time around.

"Right! For Ice Cream Kid!" he responded.

"Ick," I mumbled.

"Does that make me your side-ick? Instead of sidekick? Because I'm not cool with that," Bert said.

Gramps wanted to know if I needed help with the tights. Boy, now there's a weird thing to hear your grandpa ask. I'm pretty sure Bert was chuckling under the covers at this. I told Grandpa I'd manage, and he headed out of the room.

It was a struggle, but I finally got the uniform on. There was even an orange mask that covered my eyes, kind of like the Lone Ranger's. I pulled on the mask and turned toward the mirror.

Other than the ICK across the chest, the outfit was pretty cool! It kind of looked like the ones those performers who dunk from trampolines at halftime of basketball games wear. I love those guys!

I took a closer look in the mirror. Now I could tell Grandma Joyce had made this superhero suit. She couldn't cook, but she could sure sew. I practiced a few action poses. Bert flew over onto my shoulder. Not sure we looked like a crime-fighting duo. More like a confused little pirate who couldn't afford a parrot.

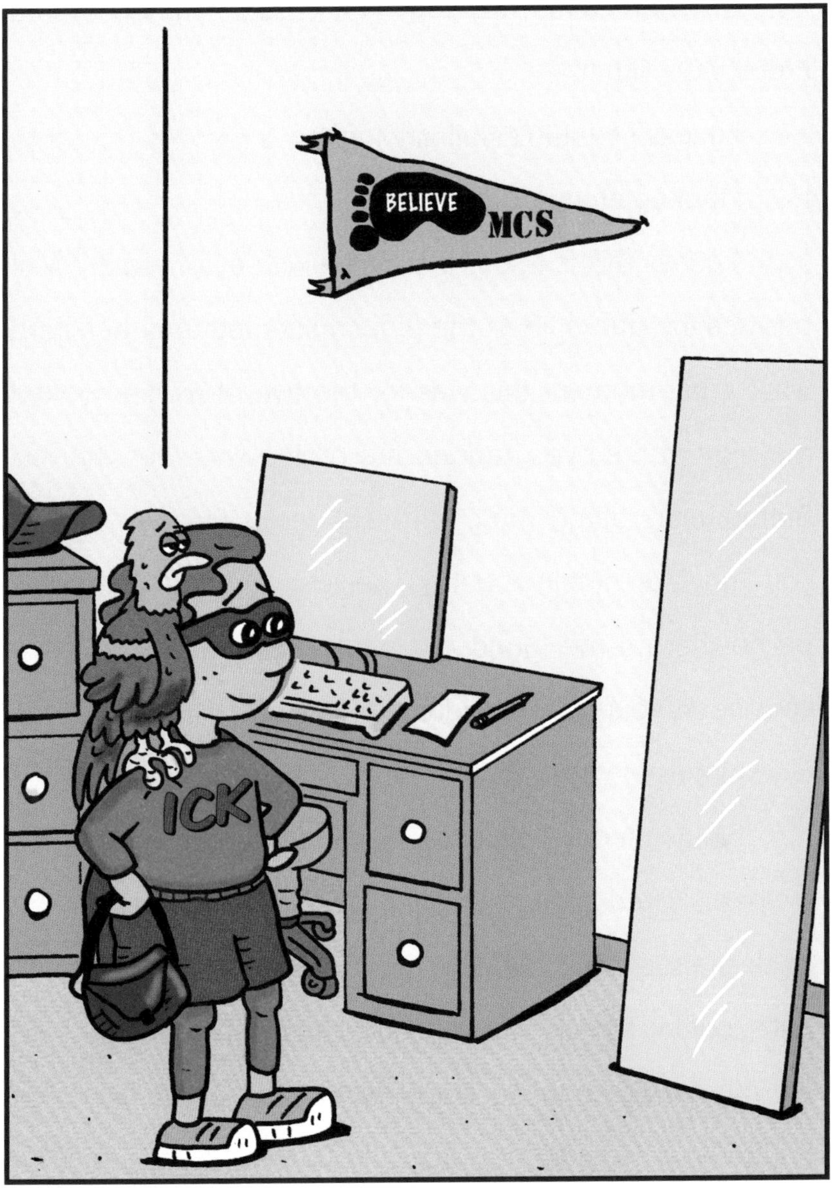
BELIEVE
MCS
ICK

Grandpa called me from downstairs: "Yo! Ice Cream Kid! It's Go Time!"

I guess I couldn't stall any longer.

I looked at my sidekick.

"I guess this is it, our first battle with evil," I said. "Well, besides the ducks." Bert the pigeon seemed to understand what a big moment this was for the two of us. He looked me right in the eyes, tapped me on the shoulder with his Butterfinger-coated wing, and said very seriously, "Just so you know, kid, if things get dangerous out there, I'm gonna be nowhere to be found. I'm a total coward. I won't have your back, your front, or your side."

Not what you want to hear from your sidekick!

We headed downstairs. The last piece of my outfit was a little insulated fanny pack to hold some ice cream bars and stuff. Grandpa was standing there, in his Mighty Super Gus outfit, putting a pack of Beech-Nut Gum into his socks. I could tell Mom was about to start crying. Dad came over and hugged me. He told me I'd be fine. Just stick with Grandpa.

"You're a Snackcracker," Dad said. "Fighting crime, and, um, accounting are what we do. Go get 'em, son."

Mom squeezed me tighter than ever, brushed some pigeon doodie off my shoulder, and ran upstairs. She didn't want me to see her cry. Although hearing her do it wasn't much fun, either.

Grandpa woke up Captain Corgi, helped him squeeze into his little outfit, which of course caused him to toot, and we were off to battle evil and save Mock City! And, as all great superheroes do, we puttered off in Grandpa's Nash Rambler.

CHAPTER 10

IT'S GO TIME

Grandpa raced the Nash Rambler through the city streets. (Well, racing for Gramps's old car was getting up to 25 miles per hour. But at least the troubled part of town was only a few minutes away.)

Our first stop was Al's Donuts, with their famous and disturbing slogan "We've got the biggest holes in town." This was where Police Chief Glazensprinkle had set up his command post. Al didn't seem too pleased. The smell of the place was amazing. I started toward a large sugarcoated bear claw, but Grandpa pulled me back.

"Maybe afterward," he said. Grandpa Gus had switched completely to Mighty Super Gus. He was serious.

I guess doughnuts could wait . . . for a little bit.

With a small, gooey clump of jelly on his face, Chief Glazensprinkle explained the situation. Bert joined the cops at the counter for doughnuts and coffee. He really seemed to blend right in.

According to the chief, Sweaty Crocker was on a crime spree downtown. Robbing from the citizens of Mock City was her way of getting revenge for being put in prison. The police had closed off a six-block area. The streets were eerily empty. It was quiet . . . too quiet. (I always wanted to say that.) Somewhere out there was Sweaty Crocker.

"I'm a little nervous about this one, Irwin," said Grandpa. "I've never gone up against her. Not sure what to expect."

I know you're probably thinking a fat old lunch lady doesn't sound too scary, but you never met Sweaty Crocker. Before getting tossed out of the school system, she'd witnessed a lot of cafeteria food fights. She knew all the tricks. Actually, most of the fights had started from her rotten cooking. Sweaty's poor work attitude and food-throwing abilities made her almost impossible to stop. We were up against a supervillain.

But we were *superheroes*.

Grandpa, Captain Corgi, Bert the pigeon, and I set out to go take back the city. I suggested we walk side by side in slow motion like they do in movie previews, with some cool song playing. Grandpa said I should just focus on staying alive.

Uh-oh. I never thought about it like that before.

Chief Glazensprinkle said one last thing before we left: "Be extra cautious, the lunch lady's not alone, she's got a sidekick."

As we got closer to the crime zone, things got pretty scary for this fourth grader. There were policemen lying all over the streets covered in blood and groaning. Captain Corgi went up and licked one.

"GROSS!" I screamed.

"Nobody gets to call *me* disgusting anymore," Bert said.

"Calm down. It's not blood, it's pasta sauce," said Grandpa.

Then he got a little on his fingertip and tasted it himself. He squinted his eyes in a disgusted way and added, "And it's the cheap stuff."

We heard some voices, and they didn't sound far away. Just as I turned to see where they were coming from, Grandpa yelled, "DUCK!"

SPLAT!

A tiny explosion hit the sidewalk right behind us.

"That's it. I'm gone," said Bert the pigeon. And he flew away . . . straight back to the doughnut command center. Grandpa said we might have to hit craigslist to find me a new sidekick. That web site has everything.

We dived, um, dove, um, jumped for cover behind a bus bench. The scent of garlic and evil was overpowering. Grandpa popped his head up real quick.

"Meatballs. From the old clock tower. So cliché."

I'd have to trust him on this one, having no idea what "cliché" means.

I grabbed the tiny binoculars from my pack and looked up at the tower. I got my first glimpse of our villain, Sweaty Crocker, with her greasy hair, and mole on her cheek. *Ewww*. She was reloading her long slotted spoon with another round of meatballs.

Captain Corgi was still eating one of the last missiles.

That dog would eat anything—even Grandma's food.

DOG THAT ONCE ATE A SHOELACE, THEN WENT BACK FOR THE OTHER ONE.

The meatballs quickly worked their ways on him. Captain Corgi farted, forcing us to change locations. Everywhere we went, Sweaty Crocker still had the advantage, because she was high above us. She could see us much better than we could see her, which didn't seem fair since we're the good guys. Splat! Zing! Whap! Things were landing all around us. A meatball hit, like, two inches from me!

"I'm scared, Grandpa!" I yelled.

He grabbed my shoulders and looked me right in the eye.

"Irwin, you're going to be fine. Now take cover behind that newspaper box!" Grandpa ripped open his pack of gum and tossed the wrapper aside. Then he went over and picked it up and put it in a trash can. He always set a good example.

And then Mighty Super Gus started chewing.

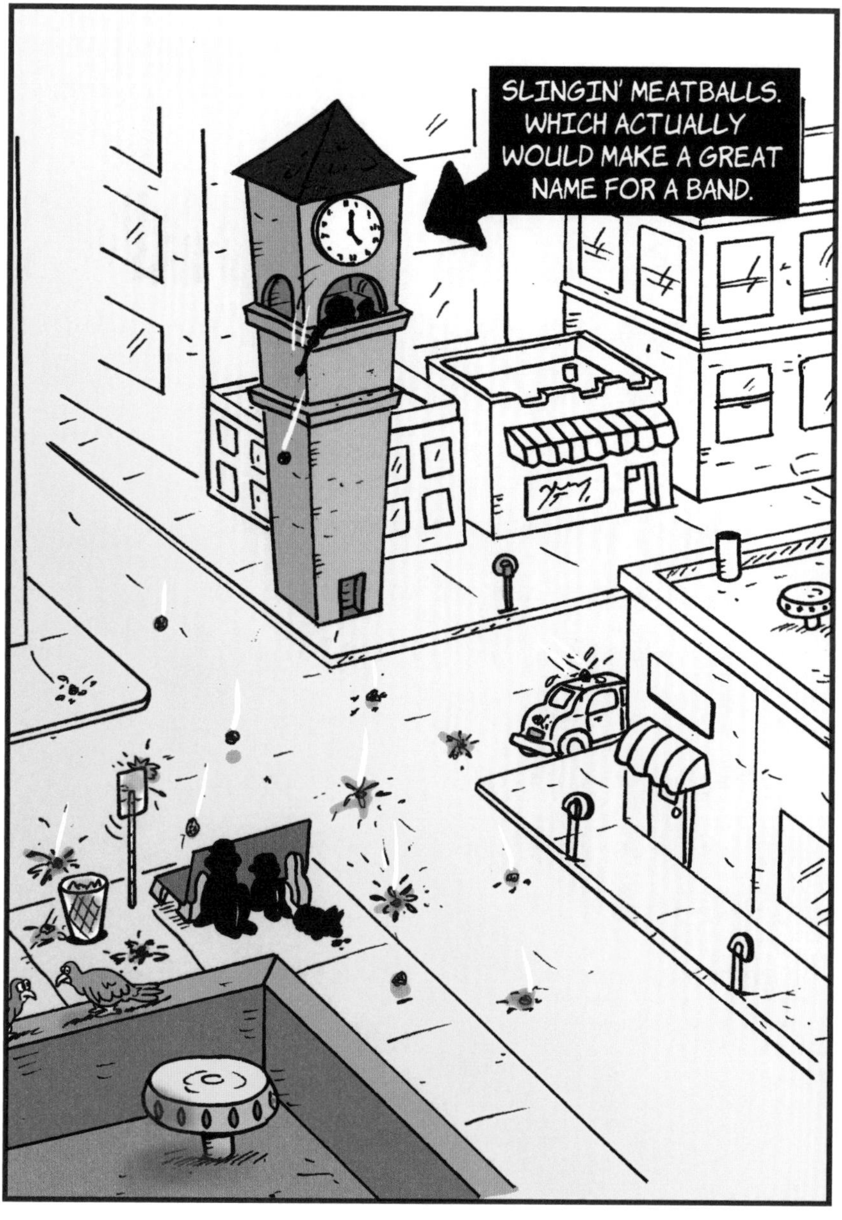
SLINGIN' MEATBALLS. WHICH ACTUALLY WOULD MAKE A GREAT NAME FOR A BAND.

CHAPTER 11

I'M TELLING ON YOU

Grandpa got a slightly crazy look in his eye. He began vibrating and then took off toward the clock tower. He moved slowly at first, and I could swear he was making those backfire noises old cars in cartoons make. But then he picked up speed. Gramps was moving! And Captain Corgi was keeping up with him! This was amazing. All these years we'd heard stories about Mighty Super Gus and his powers, and there he was! AND HE WAS MY GRANDPA!

The two of them made it to the base of the clock tower. Sweaty Crocker couldn't see them from her spot up above.

"Where'd you go, you losers?" she yelled.

Name calling is never cool.

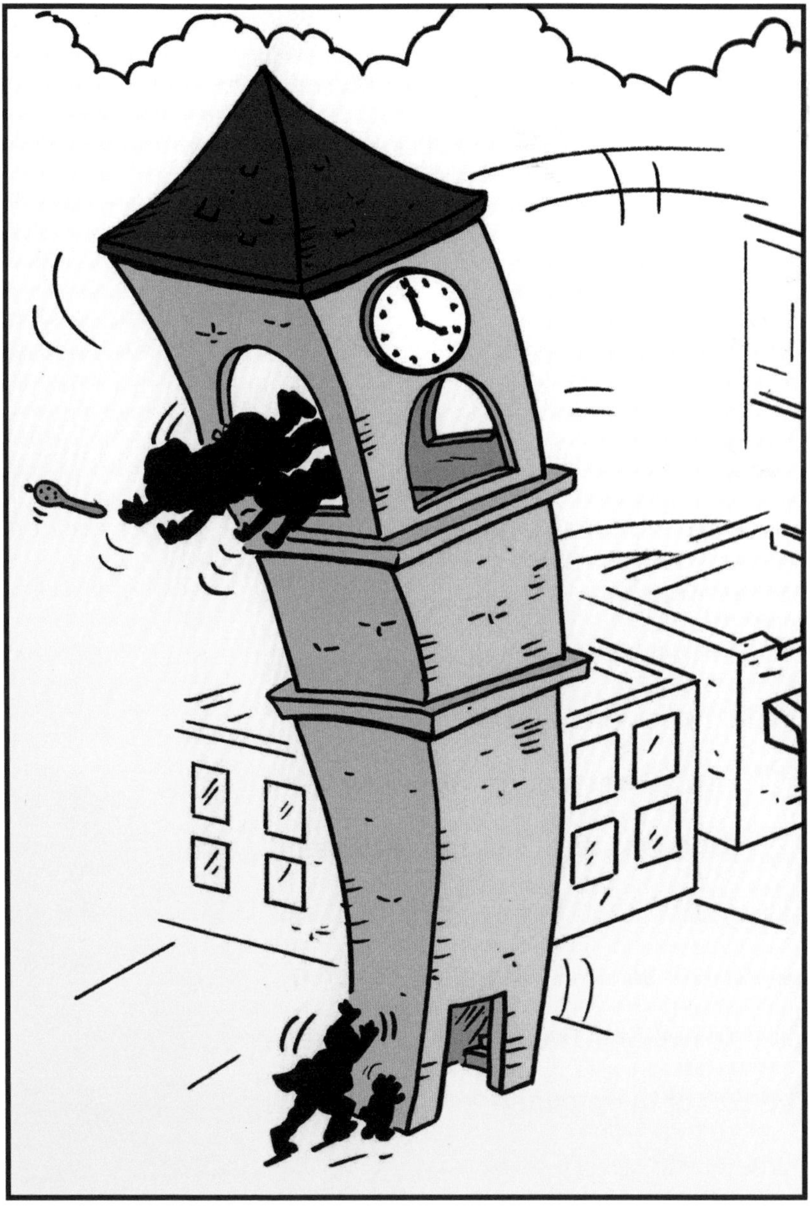

Then Grandpa's super strength kicked in. He grabbed hold of a brick corner and shook the clock tower with all his might. Sweaty Crocker started to lose her balance.

She wobbled . . .

and then wobbled some more . . .

and then she fell over the edge.

Sweaty Crocker was falling straight to the ground! Man, this was going to make a HUGE pothole! Then I noticed something else.

Sweaty Crocker wasn't alone! A tiny lunch lady was holding her hand and falling with her! She had a mask on, so I couldn't get a good look at her.

I thought they were both goners for sure. And then, just a few feet before the big and little lunch ladies splattered all over the gum-covered sidewalks of Mock City, WHOOSH! Their hairnets opened up into parachutes! The two of them glided to a hard, but safe, landing. (Which actually was pretty cool!)

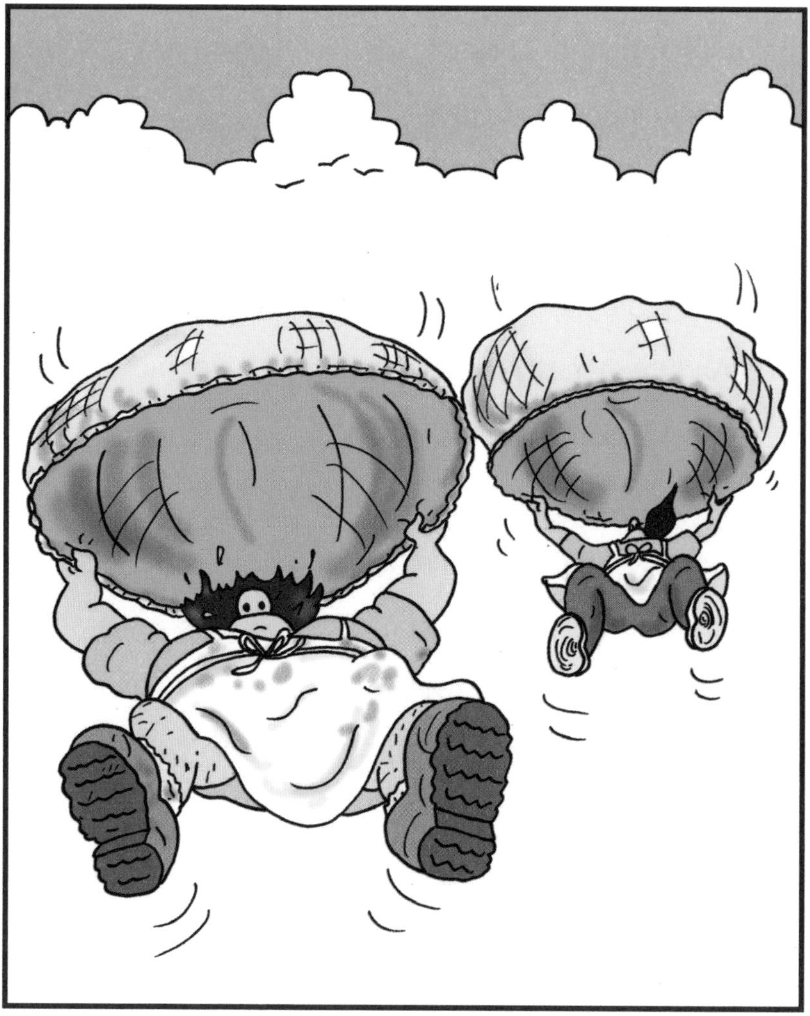

Then the little lunch lady did something strange. Before she put her hairnet back on, she did a big ol' hair flip!

Could it be?

It had to be.

I've seen that stupid hair flip a hundred times over the past few years. Nobody else in town flipped their hair like that! And the name! Of course, she only went by an initial.

The '**C**' stood for Crocker.

The little lunch lady was really a lunch *girl*: Wendy '**C**'! And her grandma was a stinky supervillain. Wendy C. must be in training with her grandma like I am with my grandpa. Wow! My real world and my work world were colliding!

The Crockers folded up their hairnets and ran right past Grandpa and Captain Corgi, who were leaning against the tower trying to catch their breath. They were too worn out from all that running and pushing to stop the archvillains. Sweaty Crocker and Wendy C. were getting away with their plastic tub full of loot!

"Hey! That's the cafeteria tub we put our dirty lunch

trays in!" I yelled. "You guys even stole the thing you're putting your stolen stuff in! That's just wrong!"

I needed to act fast. Was I ready to try something by myself? I was only, like, ten minutes into my crime-fighting career! I looked over to Grandpa, and he winked and gave me a thumbs-up. I unzipped my fanny pack (really need to come up with a better name than that) and pulled out a fudgesicle.

When I looked up again, the villains were already two blocks away. Man, that big old lady in corrective shoes could move! I chomped down into the fudgesicle. The freeze hit me, I started shaking, and ZOOM! I took off like a thousand guinea pigs all rolled into one! Wait, not guinea pigs. What was that fast animal Ms. Frost taught us about? Cheetahs! Yeah! I was running like a thousand cheetahs rolled into one.

The buildings were a blur as I ran. At probably 300 miles per hour, the only thought I had was: "Don't run into a parking meter. That would suck."

I caught up to Sweaty Crocker and Wendy C. in, like, two seconds. They were right in front of me!

Unfortunately, I still hadn't figured out how to stop.

I blew right past them at top speed. That probably looked pretty stupid. I panicked, but I managed to yell, "Halt! Or I'll, um, run past you in the other direction!"

Man, that was lame. I looked up just in time to see I was headed right for the big fountain in the town square.

SPLASH!

I went in hard and came up next to some ducks swimming in the fountain, which smelled like the city swimming pool and was kind of warm, like the shallow end where the kindergarteners swim . . . and pee. Gross. I looked back and could see Grandpa and Captain Corgi coming, but not the bad guys, er, gals.

I reached down into the water, yanked open my Superhero Tool Belt of Doom (trying out new names for the fanny pack), and grabbed an ice cream sandwich. I ripped open the wrapper. I was hoping it would still let me talk to animals. I sunk my teeth in and right away started to tingle. I turned to a duck and asked in my most confident voice, "Did you see which way those hairnetted villains went?"

JERKY DUCK...
NOT TO BE
CONFUSED WITH
DAFFY DUCK.

The duck looked at me and said, in a very jerklike way, "Why does your little yoga outfit say 'ICK' on the front?"

"It's not a little yoga outfit!" I barked. "It's clearly a superhero costume!" Man, I was *really* starting to hate ducks. Luckily, one of Mock City's giant friendly rats overheard my question and said, "There they go. On that sweet-looking hot dog cart."

I turned and saw Sweaty Crocker and Wendy C. race by a few blocks away. They had one of those food vendor's umbrella carts—with a huge engine on it. Ya' know, for bad guys they had some pretty dang sweet stuff.

Grandpa and Captain Corgi were racing behind them, huffing and puffing, and getting close. While Wendy C. drove the hotdog hotrod (which was highly illegal since she's the same age as me), Sweaty Crocker reached in her apron and pulled out a HUGE soup ladle!

"GRANDPA!" I screamed. "Look out!"

Sweaty squinted her beady eyes, took aim, and started slinging something at them. They were huge, weird-looking objects. I took a quick bite of my ice cream, and my super-vision kicked in. Cool! I've got super-vision! Now I could see that the wicked lunch lady was firing . . . *tater tots*! This REALLY made me mad!

"Hey, Crocker!" I hollered. "Tater tots weren't meant for evil! They are a force for good in the world!"

I needed speed. I reached into my pack for some fudgesicle. I planned on going so fast I could do, like, a slow-motion cartoony thing and catch the tater tots in midair. Heck, maybe the Crockers' cart even had ketchup, and I could eat a few. It was about time for my afternoon snack.

I took a big bite of chocolate power and started a new freeze. Right then I saw Grandpa and Captain Corgi both get hit by a huge barrage of tots. They went down hard.

And I went from scared to freaked!

CHAPTER 12

THEY'RE GETTING AWAY

Focus, Irwin, focus.

I knew this time I had to really try and control my speed. A quick bite of ice cream, I got tingling and took off toward Sweaty Crocker and Wendy C. I was still about fifty yards away when I reached top speed, so I jumped up and stuck my feet out in front of me, kung fu style. I flew through the air the rest of the way, and karate-kicked the hot dog cart! Food, jewelry, silverware, and ketchup bottles went flying everywhere. I had two immediate thoughts:

1. That was a supercool move on my part.

2. I'm pretty sure I just broke my big toe in about five places.

I looked back to Grandpa and Captain Corgi. Grandpa was hurt, but he gave me another thumbs-up. Man, I just realized what a tough guy Mighty Super Gus is. Sweaty and Wendy were staggering up from the wreckage of the cart. Now was my chance! I needed to say something that would scare them into giving up.

"Give it up, Wendy . . . or I'll tell the principal!"

Dang. Lame again. Nobody likes a tattletale.

"*Irwin Snackcracker*? You dorkasaurus!" Wendy C. replied. "You can't stop me and Grandma Sweaty."

"Oh, and nice butt bag, loser," she added. "Goes great with your yoga outfit."

"It's a fanny pack! I mean . . . it's a Macho Man Pouch!" I shot back.

While Wendy C. and I argued, Grandpa Gus snuck up behind her granny. He jumped her, and next thing I knew, Mighty Super Gus and Sweaty Crocker were locked in hand-to-hand combat!

It was kind of disturbing to watch older people brawl.

After each punch or kick they stopped to complain about a certain pain or body ache. They called A LOT of time-outs. Captain Corgi limped over to the action. He was hurt, but did what he could to help. He farted, which actually helped nobody. Bless his heart for trying.

Sweaty reached deep inside her apron and pulled out another soup ladle. She clocked Grandpa Gus upside the head! Captain Corgi bit her ankle, but she smacked him, too.

I was panicking! I wasn't helping the situation at all! Wendy C. kicked me in the shin and flipped her hair, which smacked me in the face! This girl was really starting to get on my nerves! She pulled out a squirt gun and cried, "Stand back, Irwin, or ICK, whatever your name is," she said. "This thing is LOADED with cootie juice!"

"WHAT? It comes in liquid form? I never knew that!" I did what she said. I backed away.

Then Wendy C. let loose with a gigantic evil laugh, which was surprisingly good for a nine-year-old girl. Sweaty had broken free from the fight with Grandpa and joined Wendy C. The two of them gathered the loot they'd stolen from banks and jewelry stores and bakeries. (Sweaty obviously enjoyed a nice cupcake now and then.) They shoved it all in a big sack and started climbing the bricks up the side of the building next to them. They looked like Spider-Man— you know, if he wore a lunch lady outfit. Sweaty yelled something about their "Grand Finale!"

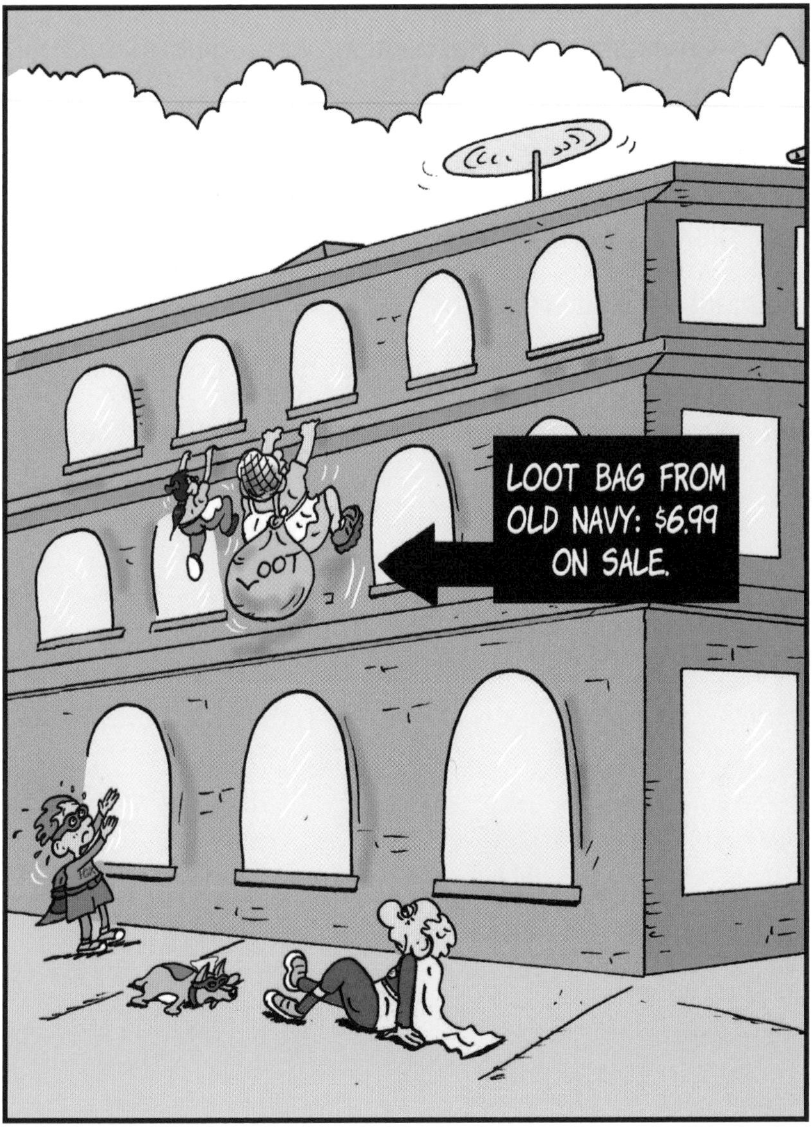
LOOT BAG FROM
OLD NAVY: $6.99
ON SALE.
LOOT

We heard chopper noises from the rooftop. Man, if those Crockers had a helicopter I was going to be mad. Why should the bad guys have all the cool stuff, while we've got a 1960 Nash Rambler? Anyhow, back to business.

Before I knew it, those crooks were halfway up the building! I looked at Gramps. He tried to get up, but was hurt too badly. I could tell it was hard for him to be seen like this, but he managed to say, "It's up to you, Irwin. Trust yourself."

CHAPTER 13

TEAM EFFORT

I unzipped my Superhero Survival Kit (still trying new names) and looked at my choices. I hadn't tried a drumstick yet. Not sure if this was the right time for experiments, but we were running out of time. I unwrapped it quickly and chomped. The brain freeze hit hard. It hurt more than the others. That really got my attention. I started shaking, but didn't feel out of control. The freeze pain slowed down. Up ahead, Sweaty and Wendy were still climbing away, faster than ever.

Then I started climbing, too.

With my drumstick-fueled superstrength, I scrambled up that building like a monkey on a mission, rapidly catching up to the villains. I was almost there . . . and my strength started draining. I started to slip! I fumbled for my pack; my other hand came off the wall! I shoved the drumstick in my mouth just as I was falling, and BOOM! Another burst. Grabbed back on and shot up the wall again.

Man, that was quick. I only got a few seconds of power from the drumstick.

I caught up to the Crockers as they reached the top of the building. I grabbed on to Wendy's ankle right before she made it over the edge. It was the first time I had touched a girl intentionally—yech. I didn't care for it.

Wendy C. swirled her head around a few times, whipping her hair back to smack me in the face. Her stupid polka-dotted hairclip hit me right on the nose, too! My first superhero blood! I felt faint for just a second.

Sweaty Crocker, who had already climbed over the edge, came back to help her granddaughter. Meanwhile, they had a chopper up there that was warmed up and waiting, its blades swinging around and around. It looked like it was made from a vendor's cart as well. Man, this lunch lady was handy with a wrench. Sweaty came right at me. That mean old ex–lunch lady reached into her apron of evil, pulled out a HUGE spatula, and took a big swipe at me! Then Sweaty stopped to let loose a crazy, evil laugh (must run in the family)—and while her mouth was wide open, something zipped right in her stinkin' pie hole.

It was a cookie!

I looked down at the street and there was Grandma Joyce! She'd flung one of her nasty cookies right at Sweaty. I think she turned one of her hair curlers into a slingshot!

"Don't mess with my boys, you witch!" Grandma yelled.

Wow. I'd never seen Grandma Joyce mean before. It was a little scary. And who knew that all this time her cooking was actually ammunition, not food?!

HAIR CURLER SLING:
DON'T MESS WITH
GRANDMA.

Now, anybody else would have spit out that nasty cookie, but Sweaty made the mistake of trying to eat it. The horrible taste stopped her in her tracks.

This gave me enough time to reach for my Insulated Pack of Problems for Bad Guys (that one might be a tad long), but Sweaty quickly recovered before I could do anything. (I guess all those years of eating her own bad cooking made her immune.) Grandma kept launching cookies, but none hit their mark. Sweaty took another swipe at me with her deadly spatula (more like the Excalibur sword from King Arthur, really), but this time she went for my bag, and cut the belt.

She knew where I was getting my superpowers!

My Superhero Tool Belt of Doom/Macho Man Pack/ Defender of Justice Bag plummeted to the ground below. There go my superhero abilities and our chances to stop the bad guys.

As I watched it fall, Wendy C. leaned over and gave me a wet willie! I didn't even know girls knew *how* to do that!

"See ya, Junior! Bye-bye, Gus!" yelled Sweaty.

She and the little lunch lady grabbed their stuff and headed for the hot dog chopper, which was only, like, thirty feet away. I tried to pull myself over the edge of the building, but I was exhausted, plus my ear hole was wet.

My first big mission, and I had failed.

I'll bet they kick you out of the superhero club for this sort of thing. I guess I still had zombie-baseball-playing-surfer dream to fall back on. This was horrible. My arms ached from hanging on to the building, and now I didn't have any source of new strength.

I looked down to the sidewalk below to see where my fanny pack landed. Maybe I could climb down, lick the pavement, and still get powers from the puddles of melted ice cream?

It was nowhere to be seen.

Weird. There should have been frozen treats scattered on the ground five floors below. Man, NOTHING was going right.

Suddenly something bonked me on the back of my head! What the heck could that be?!

It was my pack! And Bert the pigeon was holding it in his filthy little doughnut-covered claws!

"Need this?" he asked.

"Bert! You came back to help! You really do care about us as a crime-fighting duo!"

"Yeah, well, Al ran out of the good doughnuts. All he had left were the plain ones. Why bother?" Bert replied.

He was one sarcastic sidekick.

CHAPTER 14

CAN WE WRAP THIS UP?

I ripped into the pack and grabbed the last of the drumstick! It was a huge chunk. I got the biggest brain freeze yet! I shook my head and launched over the ledge onto the building's rooftop! I had new energy! New focus! Nothing could stop me now!

"Well, look who's back for more!" yelled Sweaty.

I looked around. Didn't see anyone.

"YOU! You little idiot! I'm talking about you!" she said.

"Oh, right," I answered. "And it's time for justice to prevail!"

Hey. I kind of liked the sound of that, but I needed a second opinion.

"Did that sound like a good catchphrase to you, Ms. Sweaty?"

"Eh, I've heard better," Sweaty Crocker replied.

Grandpa and Captain had rallied and were right behind me coming over the edge of the roof.

"Step away from my grandson, Sweaty!" yelled Mighty Super Gus.

The lunch lady reached down one more time into her apron. She pulled out a steaming pan of fresh meat loaf!

"My word!" I yelled. "How much stuff does that apron hold?"

"Stand back! I'm not afraid to use this. It sent one kid to the hospital just for smelling it," she snarled.

"Do what she says, butt-bag boy," added Wendy C. "My grandma's cooking is the worst!"

"Thank you, dear," said Sweaty.

"Well, I'm not so sure. *My* grandma's cooking is pretty

rotten as well. But we can argue about that another time,"
I said.

Sweaty loaded up her serving spoon and hurled it at
Gramps and Captain.

WHAP! They both got hit with a meaty slice. I did the
only thing I could do. I ran around screaming while I tried to
get to my fanny pack.

Gramps was struggling. I went to help him up, and
turned my back on the bad guys for just a second. You
should NEVER do that.

"Watch out!" yelled Grandpa.

Sweaty was holding a massive tube on her shoulder.

"Here comes the hairnet launcher nine thousand!"
she screamed.

WHOOMP!

We were trapped in a gigantic filthy hairnet! The thing
smelled like my baseball socks, and that's not pleasant. The
Crockers had plenty of weapons, and we were empty. My
pack was still on the ledge, twenty feet away, and Gramps

was out of gum. Wendy C. took the opportunity to poke me with a stick she found on the roof. She was NOT going to be on my birthday party list.

While we squirmed inside that funky hairnet, Sweaty Crocker pulled out a control box and howled:

"MOCK CITY WILL NOW FEEL MY WRATH! I WILL DESTROY THIS PLACE WITH . . . **CHOPTIMUS GRIME**! THE MOST WICKED KITCHEN GADGET THE WORLD HAS EVER SEEN!"

Well, I gotta admit, that piqued my interest.

Sweaty started furiously pushing buttons on the control box. Then she pointed her unwashed finger toward Mock City School, off in the distance.

"Behold!" she cried.

"What?" me and Grandpa both yelled. "We can't see anything from down here."

"Oh, for crying out loud," Sweaty moaned. "Quit whining."

"Well, we can't 'BEHOLD' anything if we can't see it!" replied Gramps.

He made a good point.

"Okay, fine, ya big babies," said Sweaty. Then she and Wendy rolled us in our netting to the edge of the building for a better view.

"Thank you," I said out of habit.

"No problem," Wendy C. replied.

I could see the top of my school. Wow, I'd never seen it from up above. Man, there had to be fifty soccer balls, red rubber balls, and footballs on that roof! Sweaty went back to her remote control box, still punching buttons furiously.

"You made me lose my place," she snapped.

We started to hear noise: cracking and creaking, which actually wasn't unusual for our school. The place was ancient. It was, like, built in the '90s or something. The school building started to shake. Little bits of it crumbled off and fell to the ground. Then, from about where I figured the cafeteria was, something HUGE started coming through the roof. I couldn't make out what it was . . . it was metal, and grease covered. Then Grandpa cried out,

"It's a giant oven!"

And it was! It was a humongous oven! And it kept rising higher and higher above the school.

The giant oven had to be five stories tall . . . most of it legs. Two red "preheat" lights glowed like scary little eyes. I could hear its angry fan come on. Its front door opened and closed and snapped like a monster, while flames shot out of its mouth!

Bad enough, right? Just wait.

Two giant arms sprang out from the sides of the oven, and both had twenty-foot-long knives in their hands. Good golly this thing was nasty . . . and amazingly cool as well. I mean, if this was a toy, I'd have been begging Mom and Dad for one. What a great way to get boys interested in cooking! Sweaty Crocker had turned the school kitchen appliance into a Transformer! And then Sweaty lifted her hairy-pitted, skin-flappy arms to the sky and yelled:

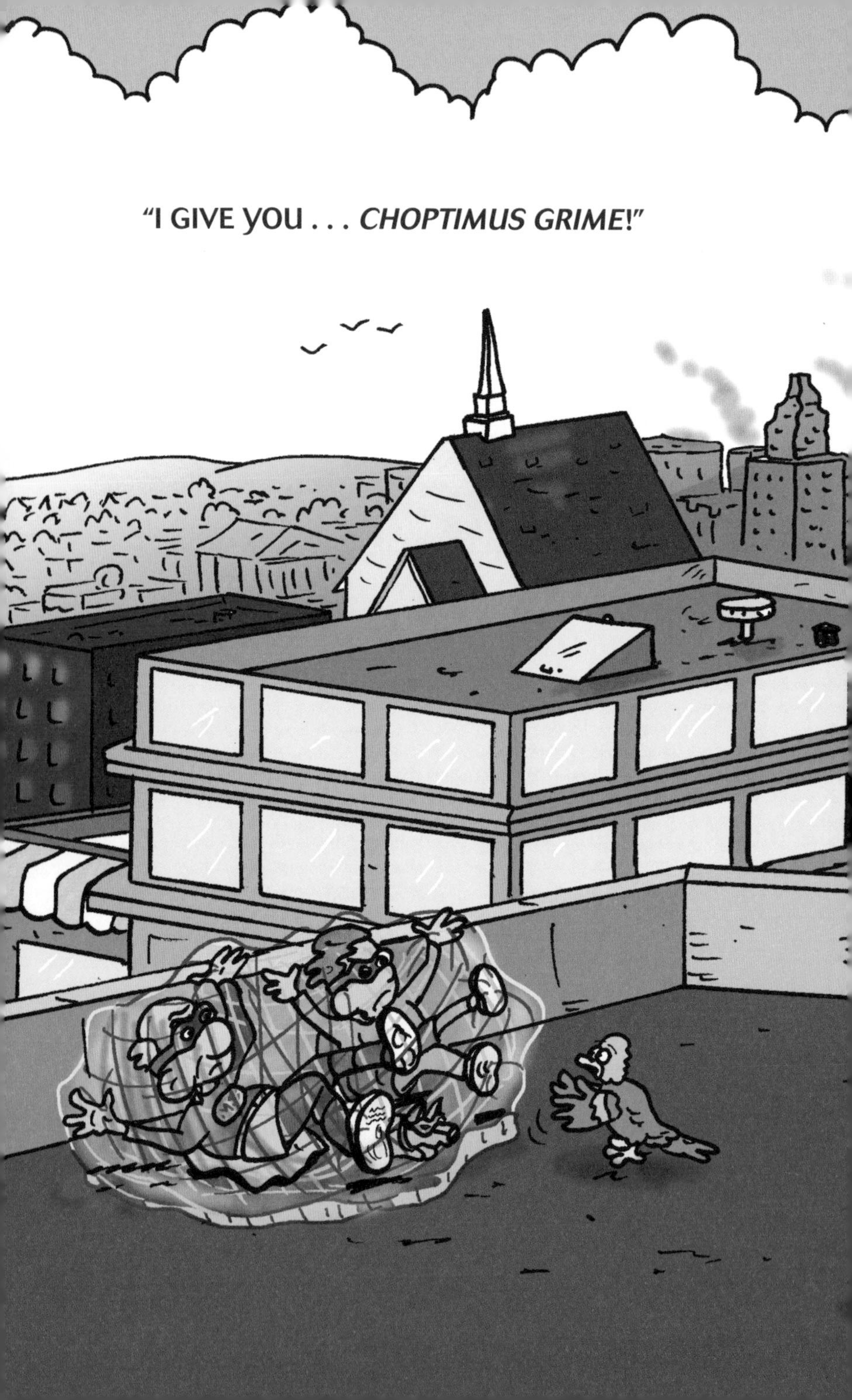

"I GIVE YOU . . . *CHOPTIMUS GRIME!*"

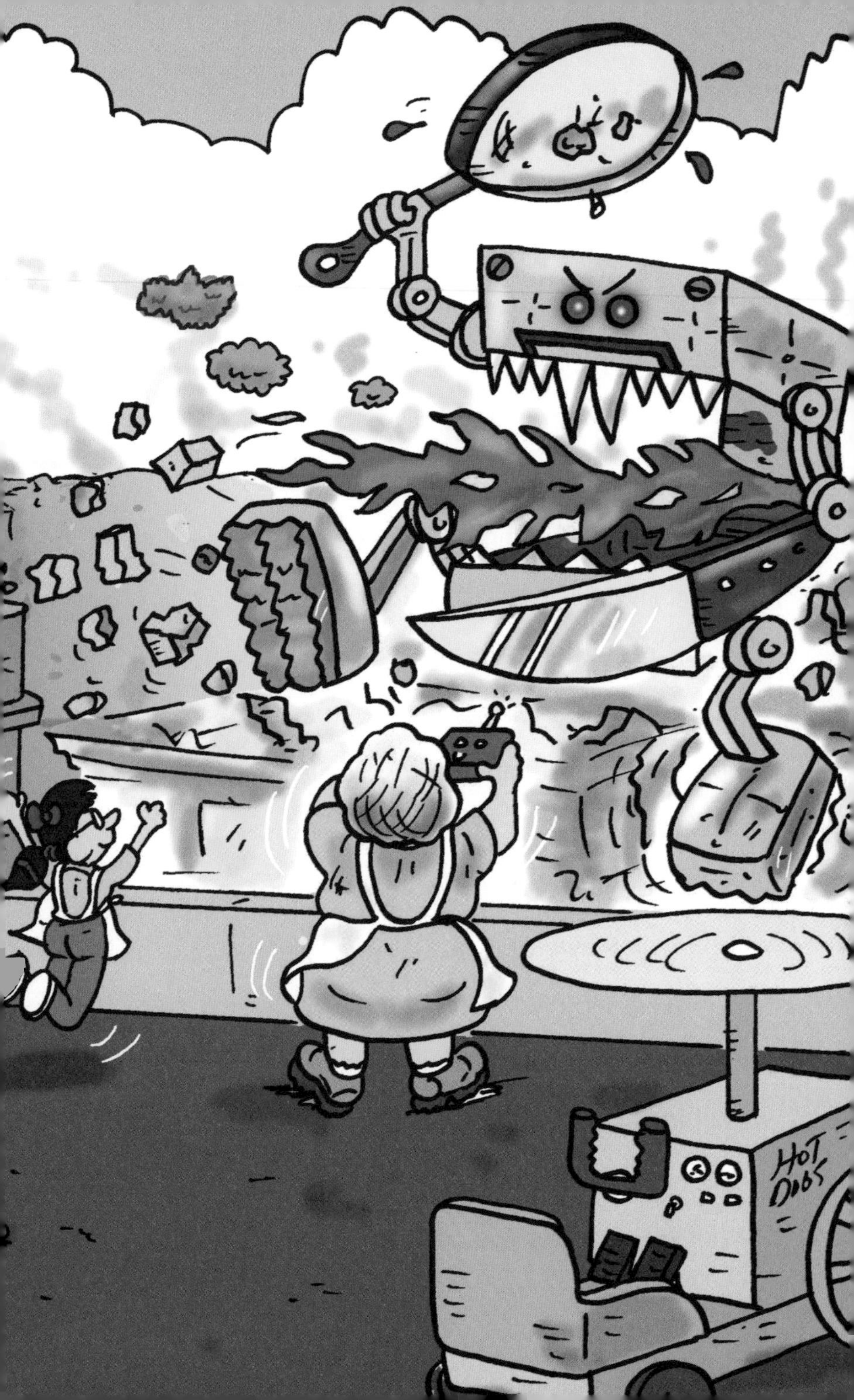
HOT DOGS

I had to give her style points for that. Very dramatic. But I also had to ask:

"If you could build this, why the heck weren't you teaching shop class?!"

With her remote, Sweaty Crocker started maneuvering this scary yet totally wicked beast toward downtown. Smash! Crash! Choptimus Grime slashed power lines and trees with its knife arms, and stomped on buildings, crushing them to rubble. Cars alarms started blaring everywhere! People ran from their homes into the streets! Cell phones snapped pictures that went immediately to Facebook.

"Mock City! This is what you get for putting horrible people in jail! Feel my wrath! Well, my cool monster's wrath!" yelled Sweaty.

Sweaty laughed with each crunch as the metal flame-snorting oven worked its way closer to where we were. She was going to crush the entire city that fired her and escape in her vendor cart chopper. If we were going to be any kind of superheroes, we needed to act fast.

Grandpa and I struggled to break free from the smelly netting; I knew I had one last ice cream in my Pouch of Doom (kind of like that one) if I could only reach it. I looked around frantically for my trusty sidekick. Captain Corgi had gotten comfortable enough under the netting I could actually hear him snoring.

"Bert! I need your help! Where are you?" I yelled.

"Yo, Irwin. I'm over here," I heard. He was back! I knew I could count on him! I saw my pigeon on the ledge, right next to my pack! Then I noticed he was busy polishing off the last ice cream I just mentioned.

BURP! My sidekick hopped over to me.

"Everything okay?" Bert asked. He had drumstick breath. "Looks kind of cramped in there."

"You gotta a beak, get us out of this hairnet," I whispered.

Sweaty and Wendy were way busy with their evil cackling and high-fiving and watching Choptimus Grime destroy Mock City. Bert went to work on the netting, and got it a little loose, when Wendy C. saw him.

"Hey! No cheating!" she cried out. "Be cool, Irwin!"

"Wendy! Go sit on them! I'm almost done here!" barked Sweaty. "Just a few more minutes to demolish Mock City! Bwahahahaha!"

Wendy C. pinned us down, taking extra joy in rubbing her butt on me! She even made up a little song, which REALLY ticked me off . . . mostly because it was kind of catchy:

"I'm rubbing my butt on Irwin, I'm rubbing my butt on Irwin. He's a stinky doodyhead, and his face is turning red."

Great. Now I'll have that song stuck in my head all day.

Bert pecked at her. But Wendy C. did her hair whip and knocked him clear across the rooftop.

Time was running out! I had to think. What could I do?

Then it hit me . . . the ultimate defense against girls of any age.

Of course!

BOOGERS!

I started wiggling my arm up close to my face. Grandpa looked at me, wondering what I was doing.

"I've got a plan," I whispered.

"No talking, Irwin!" Wendy C. barked.

I moved my arm slowly upward. Across my chest, under my chin, over my totally dry mouth . . . I was almost there. My nostril was so close. Just a little farther. I could see Choptimus Grime getting closer to us, and hear buildings crunch and Mock City citizens screaming for help. I made it to my nose. I dug in the right side, which is usually my go-to nostril. Dang! Not much there. I shifted over to lefty . . . and scored a gem!

I pulled the snot out carefully. I couldn't risk dropping it, this nose nugget just might save our city.

I was inches from Wendy C.'s leg when I cried out, "Ohhh, Weeeendy! Looky what I got."

Wendy C. turned and saw my loaded finger

"Back off, Wendy. I got nothing to lose. I'll wipe this right on your . . ."

"AAAAUUUUGGGGHHHH!" she screamed and ran across the rooftop.

"BOOGER!"

"WHERE?!" asked Sweaty. "Settle down, Wendy!"

While Wendy C. was screaming and Sweaty was scolding, I managed to open the netting a little more and wiggle out. Then I pulled Grandpa through, too. Bert was getting back up on his chubby little legs, and Captain was stretching after a nice, solid nap under the netting. I chased after Wendy C. and just about ran right into Sweaty's filthy apron. She hadn't moved. She stood still and pointed at my finger.

"Drop the booger!" she demanded.

"Never!" I fought back.

"Why are you doing this, anyway?" I yelled.

"Because of little brats like you! Little brats who got sick from my cooking!"

"So why not just get another job?!" I screamed.

"Because the Crocker family cooks! That's what we do! Do you know what it's like to have a famous cooking sister?"

"Who's your sister?" I asked.

"Betty Crocker! I think she invented instant mashed potatoes!"

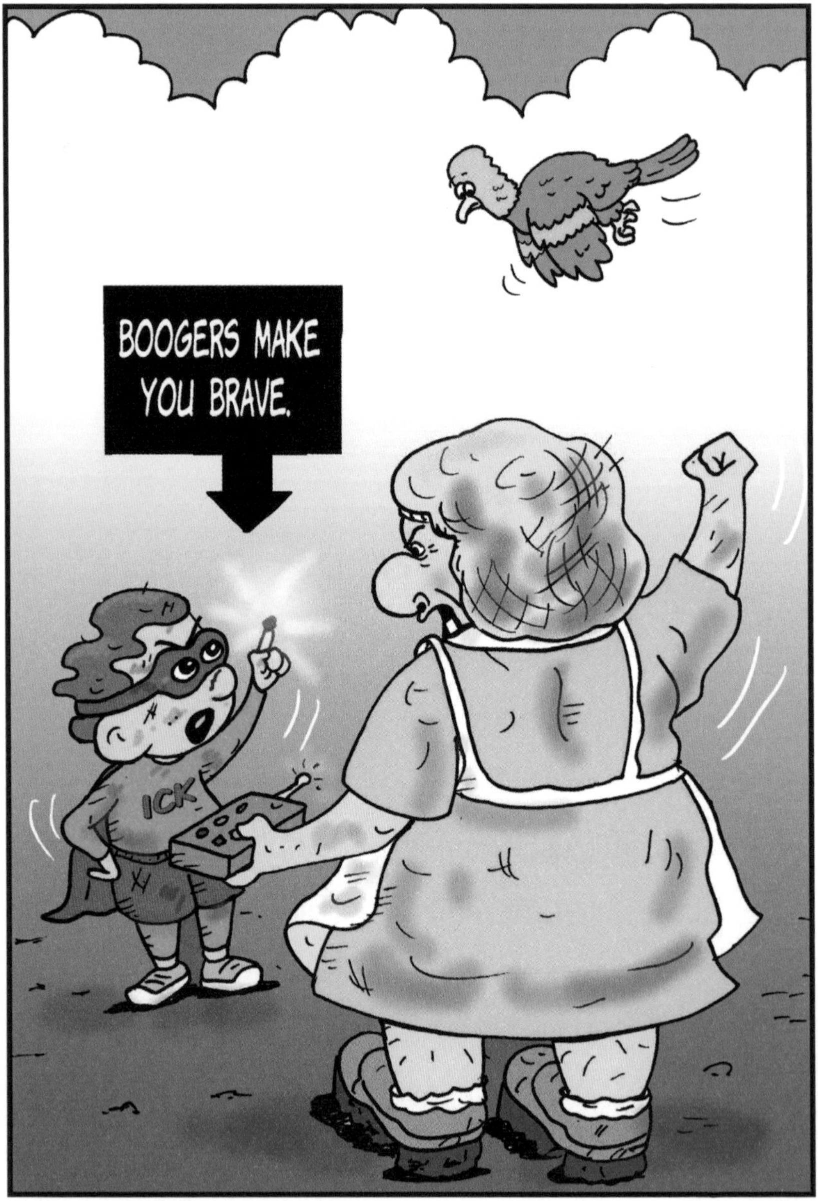
BOOGERS MAKE YOU BRAVE.
ICK

"Ooh. I love those," I said. "But that's no excuse for what you did! You nearly killed four kids! I think you deserved some punishment!"

I was surprised at how I stood up to this archvillain. Sweaty was clearly getting angry. She reached into her apron for something to clobber me with, and in that one second dropped the remote. It tumbled across the roof.

"Bert! Grab the remote!" I yelled. The pigeon swooped down and grabbed it! Sweaty cursed and reached up to grab it back, but Bert was too fast! I kicked her in the shin. She dropped to the rooftop, yelling at me for not being respectful to adults. Bert flew over and dropped the remote into Grandpa's hands.

"Good work, you two!" yelled Grandpa. "Now, anybody have a clue how to operate this thingee?" he asked as he stared at the remote.

Grandpa started pushing buttons as fast as he could.

"Nope. That one's Facebook. Nope. That one turned on the monster's MP3 player."

"Grandpa! Try the red one!" I yelled.

He pushed it, and Mighty Super Gus shut down the monster right before it took out our city's most valuable asset . . . the comics bookstore. Close call. Grandpa usually took quite a while to figure out gadgets. But that's what makes him Mighty Super Gus. He comes through when he needs to. The police force made its way onto the roof right then. Sweaty Crocker got handcuffed, vowing even bigger revenge when she got out of jail.

Mock City saved.

CHAPTER 15

ENDING JUNK

The following Monday at school, I tried to act normal. There was a picture of me and Grandpa and Captain Corgi in the paper. So far, no one had said anything to me about it. I guess they didn't recognize me in my ICK outfit. I knew it would happen: I ran into Wendy C. in the hallway.

"Hello, Wendy." I said. "Have a nice weekend?"

"It's Wendy C., and you know it, Irwin the butt-bag boy."

"From now on, I'm just calling you Wendy. Unless you want me to tell everyone about your evil grandma."

"You do that, and I'll tell everyone your grandpa is Mighty Super Gus."

She was good.

"Fine, Wendy C. it is." I said.

"So, I guess we have a pact about keeping our identities secret?" she asked.

"I guess so," I said.

I definitely didn't want everyone to know what Grandpa and I had going on with the superhero stuff. I hated making a deal with a girl like Wendy C., but I sort of had to. Plus, it was kind of cool to get that first lifelong enemy under my belt. We shook hands and swore to destroy each other . . . and went about our business.

With all the excitement, and kids being disappointed school wasn't closed since it had a massive hole in it, I thought Ronnie Herzog might have forgotten about our bet. He hadn't. After school, the race with Elisha was on. The playground was packed.

I think half the school was there to watch. I felt sick. I thought about getting an ice cream for superspeed, but I'd promised Grandpa the brain freezes were to be used only for crime fighting. I'd sworn on it.

I was sweating, and my mouth was so dry I couldn't stand it. I saw that Trey had a beverage.

"Dude, let me have a drink. My mouth is totally dry." I said.

"No way. I don't want your gross lips on my straw. That's disgusting," he answered.

"TREY! I'm dying here. C'mon!"

"All right . . . but you owe me for this," he said, and then handed me his drink. I took a deep slurp of . . . cherry slushie.

It wasn't exactly ice cream, but it was enough to give me a slight brain tingle.

We walked to the starting line drawn in the dirt. Elisha smiled at me.

"Isn't this fun?" she giggled.

Someone yelled "GO!" and we took off. Elisha took a slight lead, but I was actually staying close . . . and then catching up . . . and then passing her right at the finish line! The slushie worked just enough to give me some speed. Or MAYBE I'd gotten faster over the last two days.

Doubtful.

Elisha was shocked. EVERYONE was shocked. The boys were going crazy. Someone had finally beaten Elisha in a race. I figured they would probably hold a parade in my honor.

Then Elisha had to go and ruin my big moment.

She *kissed* me and said, "Good race."

AAUUGGHH! Good sportsmanship and a smooch. This was horrible. At least Ronnie looked pretty green.

I kept wiping off my cheek while Trey, Elisha, and I walked home. Elisha would NOT stop talking about the superhero-supervillain showdown. It's not like it was that big of a deal. Seemed like Mock City was always in some sort of weird trouble. That's what kept Mighty Super Gus in business all these years. But apparently this latest episode wasn't handled the way she and the Firecamp Scouts would have handled it. I tuned out until she said, "I heard that little crime-fighter boy has super farting power. Isn't that gross?!"

"I, uh, heard that was the dog," I mumbled.

Trey had been pretty quiet the whole time. Just kind of listening and "uh-huhing" in agreement now and then. We got to Elisha's house, and she skipped up the steps

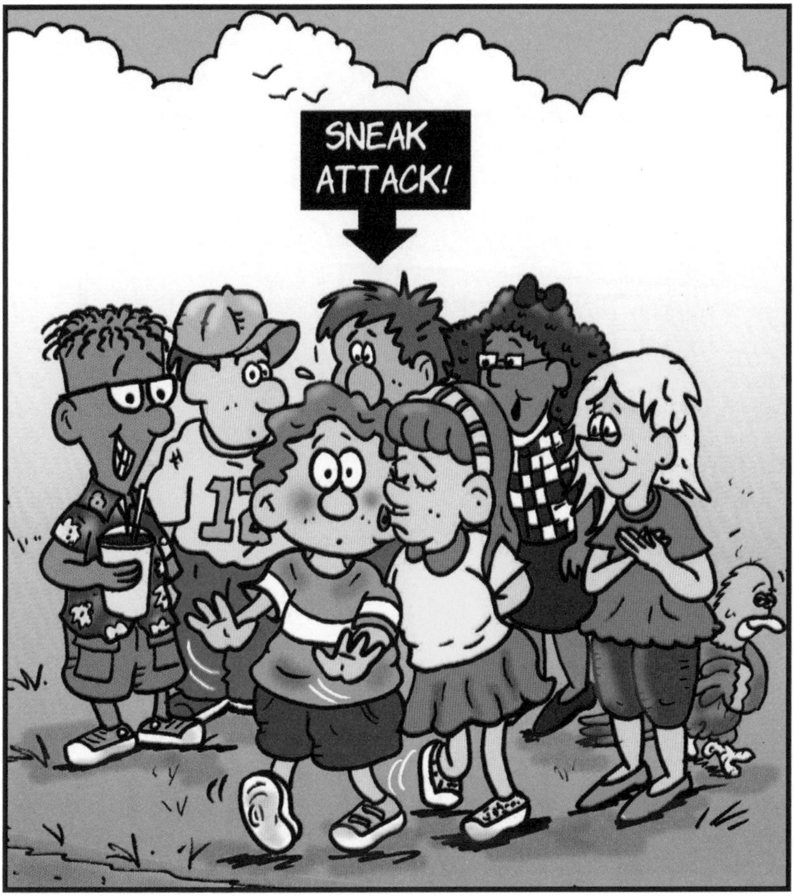
SNEAK ATTACK!

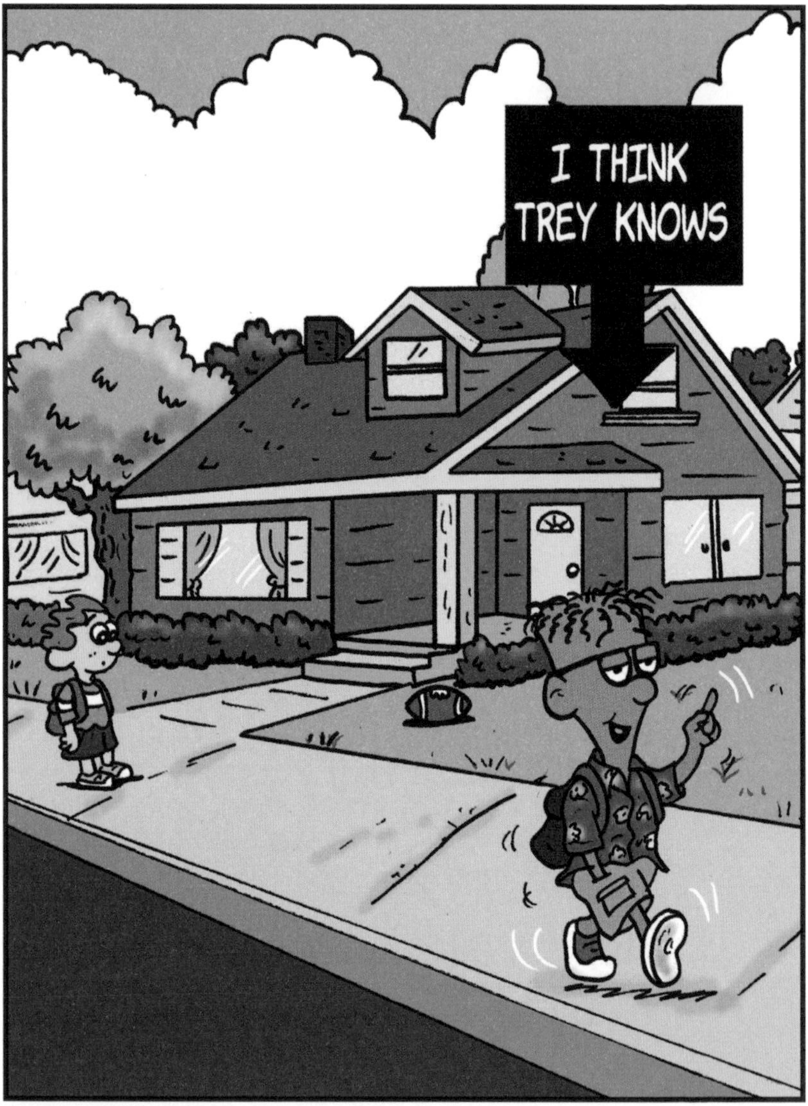
I THINK TREY KNOWS

and disappeared inside. Strange how someone could be so happy after just losing a race. I guess that's a big difference between boys and girls. Those things don't bother them like they do us.

Trey and I kept walking. He finally got in one shot about the kiss, calling me "lover boy." We came to my house and I headed up the walkway, exhausted after the last couple of days of nonstop action.

"Later, dude," I said to Trey as he kept going.

Then, I think . . . I'm not sure . . . but I thought I heard him quietly say, "If that pigeon doesn't work out as a sidekick, you know where to find me."

Crud.

Trey knows.

THE END

MORE
TO EXPLORE!

Hey, guys! It's me, Irwin! You're not quite done yet! These next couple pages have some cool stuff on them for you to learn! Don't worry; there won't be a test on it. Just bonus fun! Like when you think you're all out of M&Ms and then find one more stuck down in the corner of the bag. Don't you love it when that happens? Have fun!

Irwin's Ice Cream List

Fudgesicle

A robust, chocolatey little treat on a wooden stick, which gives the power of superspeed, and brief ability to talk with animals. Perfect for after a grossest booger contest.

Ice Cream Sandwich

A modest brain-freezer with big results. It gives top speed, which lasts longer than you'd expect, improved vision, and the understandment of critters. Also, the chocolate crust sticks to your fingers, providing a snack for later in the day.

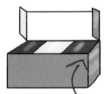

Drumstick

A nutty, bold gem of an ice cream. Gives a very quick burst of strength and energy. Goes perfectly with an afternoon of fighting evil girls from your class.

That means you, Wendy C!

Neopolitan

Although not convenient for fighting criminals in the field, this triple threat combo is a long-standing favorite with moms. It combines three unique ice creams in one daring carton.

Eating the strawberry is totally optional.

Popsicle

This frozen, flavored water on a stick seems simple enough, but these little beauties give me the power of . . . oh, sorry, that's the next book.

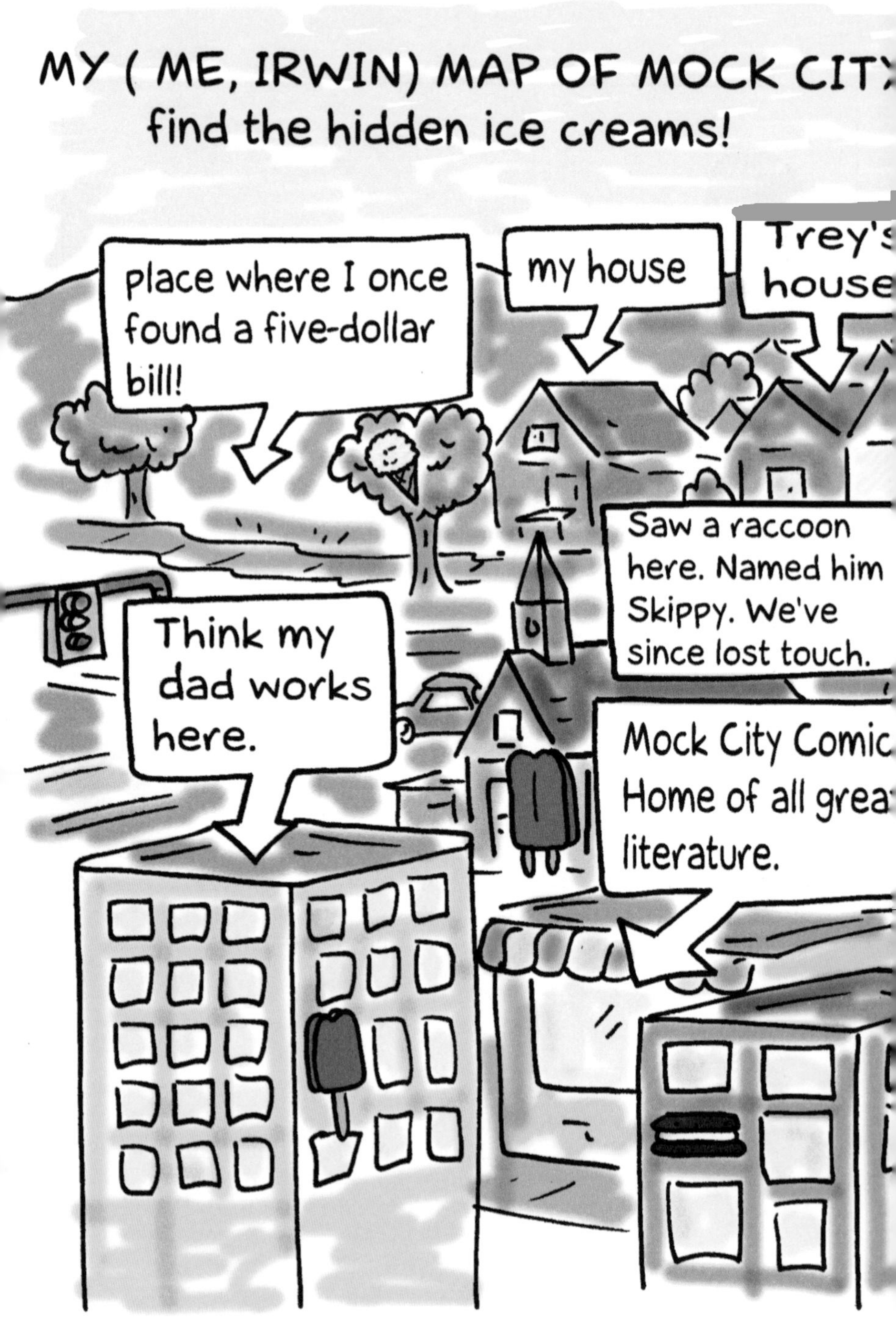
MY (ME, IRWIN) MAP OF MOCK CIT
find the hidden ice creams!
place where I once found a five-dollar bill!
my house
Trey's house
Saw a raccoon here. Named him Skippy. We've since lost touch.
Think my dad works here.
Mock City Comic
Home of all grea
literature.

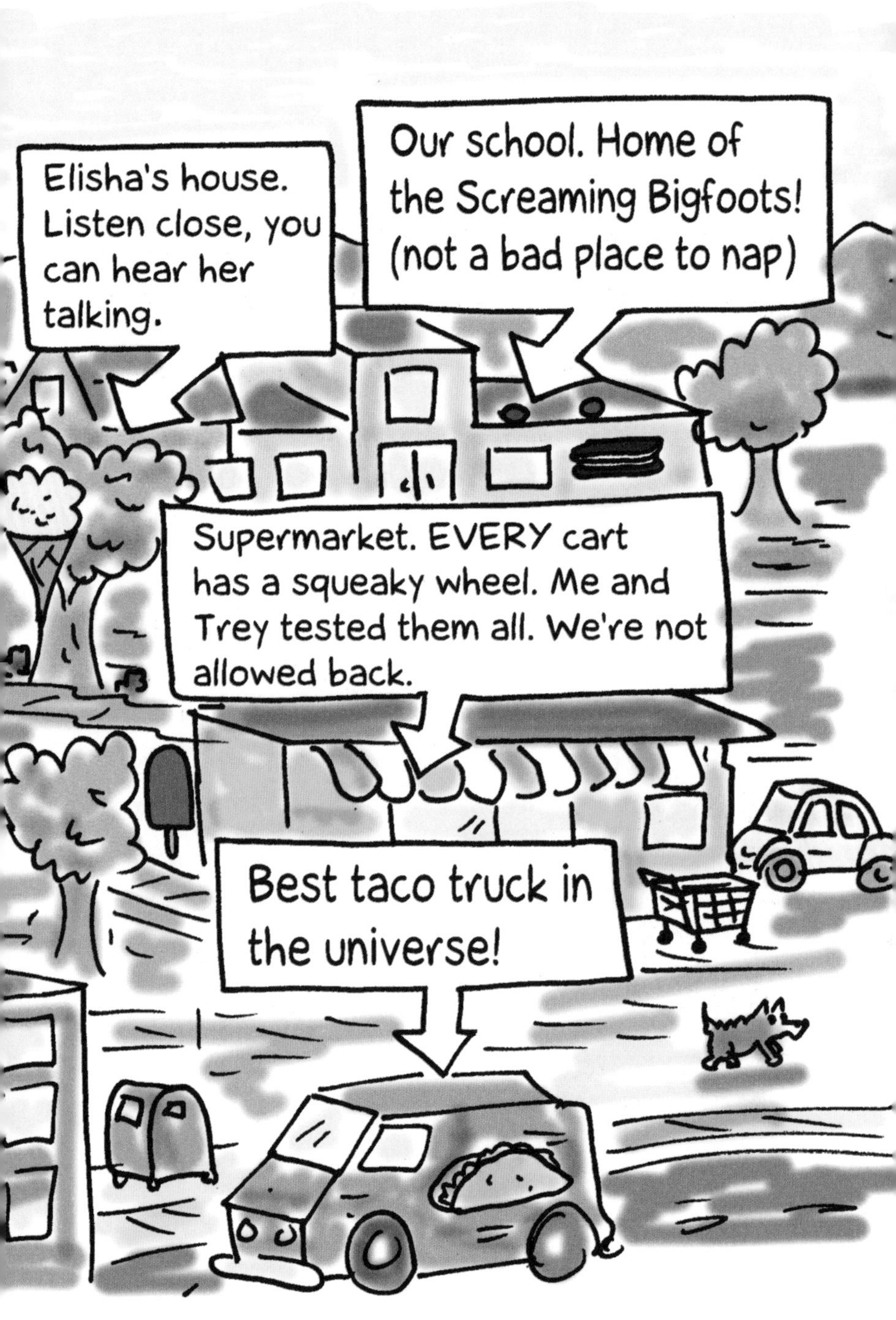
Elisha's house. Listen close, you can hear her talking.
Our school. Home of the Screaming Bigfoots! (not a bad place to nap)
Supermarket. EVERY cart has a squeaky wheel. Me and Trey tested them all. We're not allowed back.
Best taco truck in the universe!

MY ~~FANNY~~... SUPERHERO TOOL BELT OF JUSTICE AND MACHO DEFENDER OF...UM, STUFF BAG.

PICTURE OF BATMAN. HE PROBABLY HAS ONE OF ME, TOO.

GRANOLA BAR PUT IN BY MOM FOR HEALTHY SNACK. OATS AND HONEY. MUST BE WHY HORSES AND BEES FOLLOW ME.

PLACE WHERE MY CELL PHONE WILL GO. IF MY MOM AND DAD EVER BUY ME ONE!

QUARTER STUCK TO POUCH. KINDA GROSS. KINDA COOL.

COOTIE REPELLENT. ALSO WORKS ON MOSQUITOS I'M TOLD.

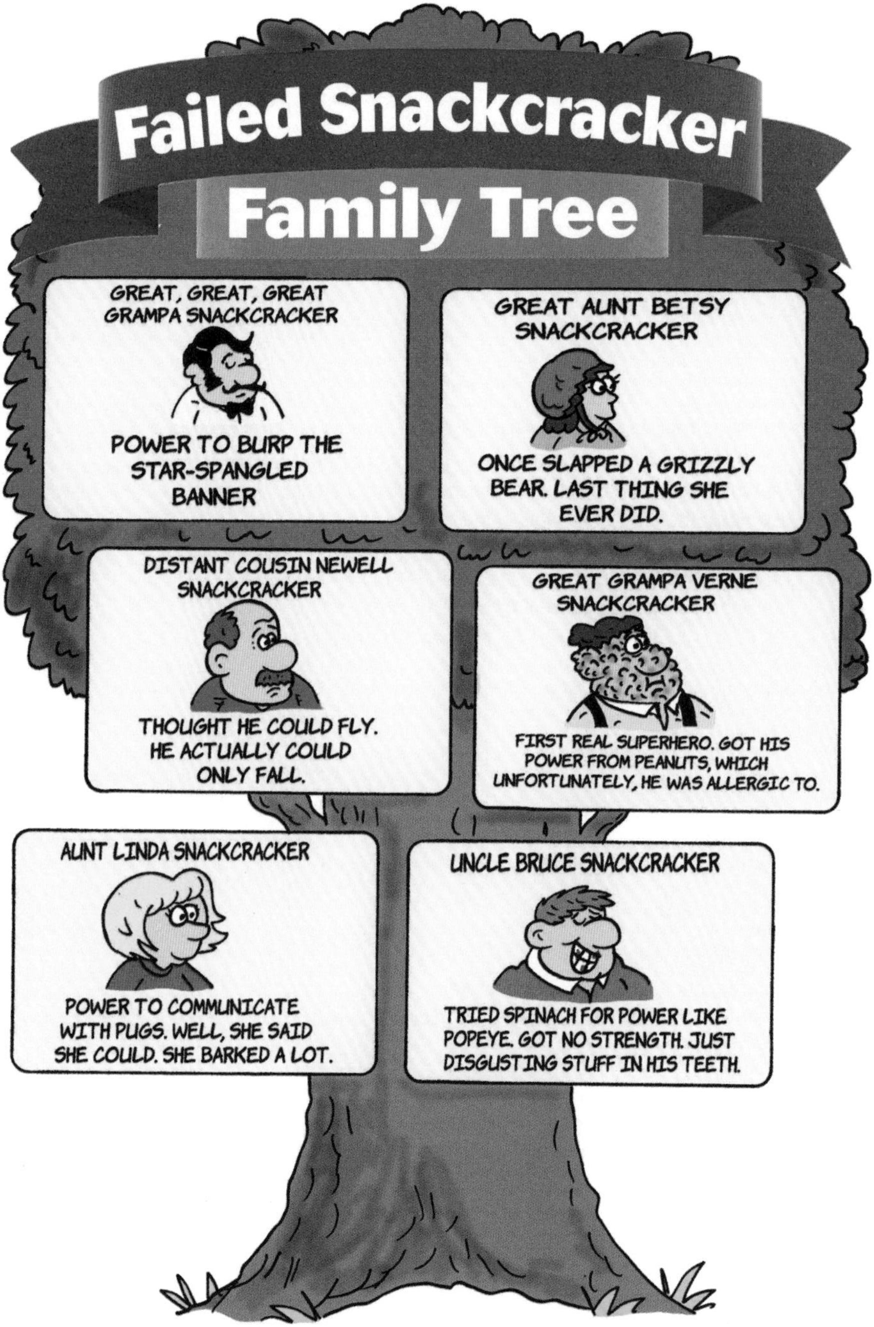
Failed Snackcracker
Family Tree
GREAT, GREAT, GREAT
GRAMPA SNACKCRACKER
POWER TO BURP THE
STAR-SPANGLED
BANNER
GREAT AUNT BETSY
SNACKCRACKER
ONCE SLAPPED A GRIZZLY
BEAR. LAST THING SHE
EVER DID.
DISTANT COUSIN NEWELL
SNACKCRACKER
THOUGHT HE COULD FLY.
HE ACTUALLY COULD
ONLY FALL.
GREAT GRAMPA VERNE
SNACKCRACKER
FIRST REAL SUPERHERO. GOT HIS
POWER FROM PEANUTS, WHICH
UNFORTUNATELY, HE WAS ALLERGIC TO.
AUNT LINDA SNACKCRACKER
POWER TO COMMUNICATE
WITH PUGS. WELL, SHE SAID
SHE COULD. SHE BARKED A LOT.
UNCLE BRUCE SNACKCRACKER
TRIED SPINACH FOR POWER LIKE
POPEYE. GOT NO STRENGTH. JUST
DISGUSTING STUFF IN HIS TEETH.

Andrews McMeel Publishing, LLC
an Andrews McMeel Universal company
1130 Walnut Street, Kansas City, Missouri 64106

www.andrewsmcmeel.com

14 15 16 17 18 SDB 10 9 8 7 6 5 4 3 2

ISBN: 978-1-4494-4424-2

Library of Congress Control Number: 2013944835

Made by:
Shenzhen Donnelley Printing Company Ltd.
Address and location of manufacturer:
No. 47, Wuhe Nan Road, Bantian Ind. Zone,
Shenzhen China, 518129
2nd Printing — 4/7/14

ATTENTION: SCHOOLS AND BUSINESSES
Andrews McMeel books are available at quantity discounts with bulk purchase for educational, business, or sales promotional use. For information, please e-mail the Andrews McMeel Publishing Special Sales Department: specialsales@amuniversal.com.

Check out these and other books at
ampkids.com

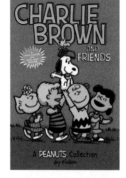

Also available:
Teaching and activity guides for each title.
AMP! Comics for Kids books make reading FUN!

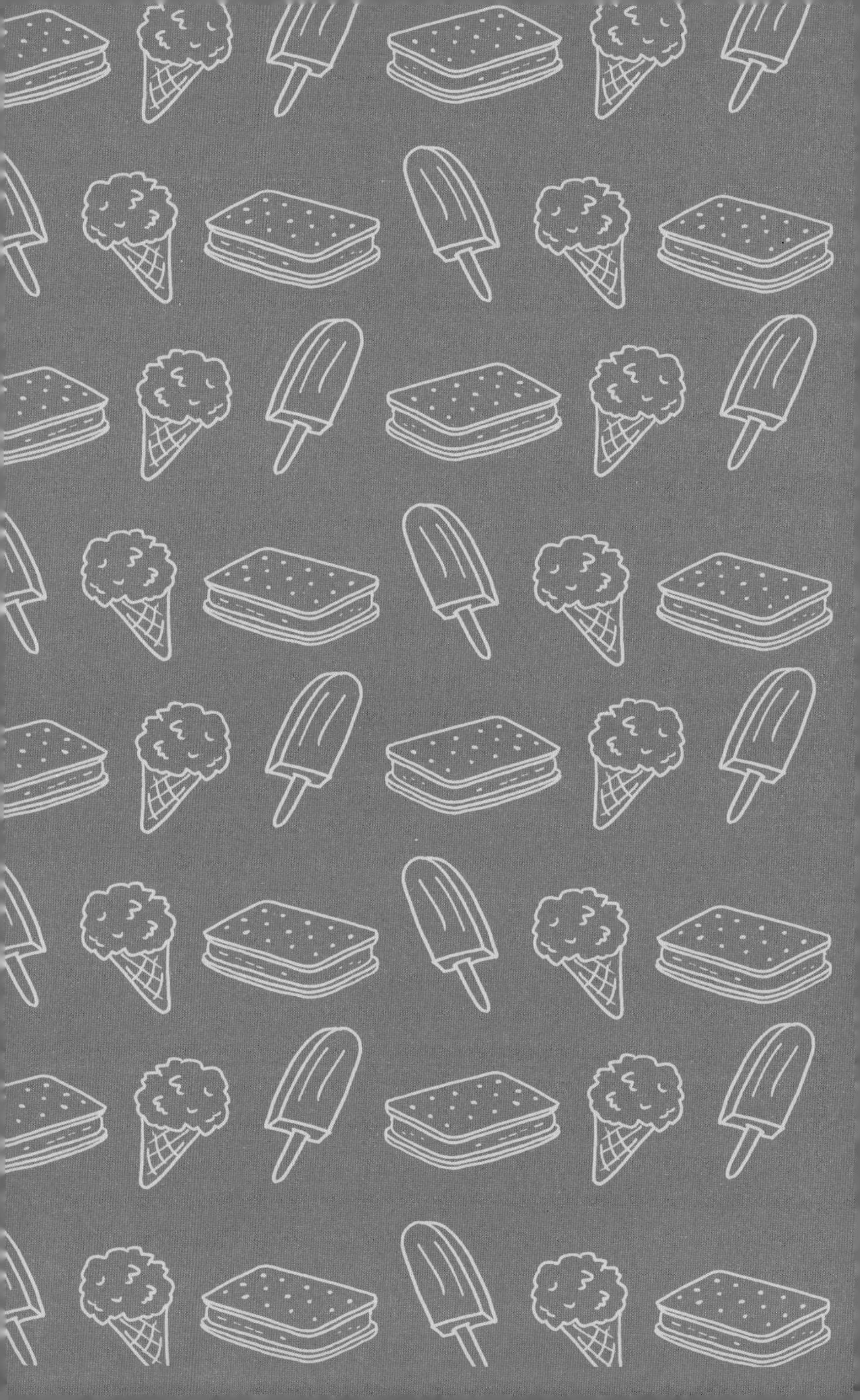

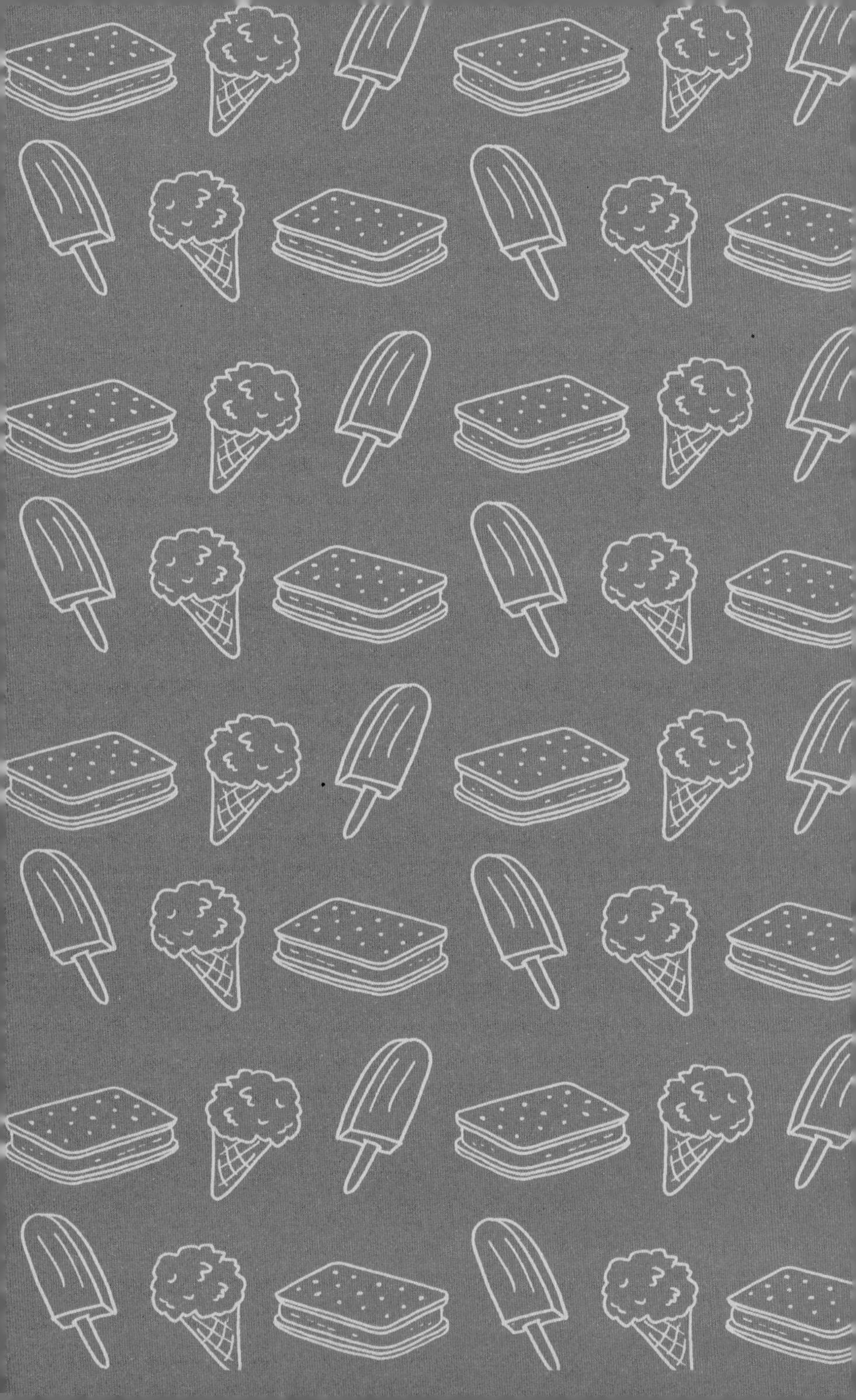